# Prudence in Hollywood
## AND OTHER STORIES

## RALPH CISSNE

# Prudence in Hollywood

## AND OTHER STORIES

## RALPH CISSNE

**M**

Library of Congress Control Number: 2019903823

ISBN-13 978-0-9998537-4-0 (paperback)
ISBN-13 978-0-9998537-5-7 (hardcover)
ISBN-13 978-0-9998537-6-4 (ebook)


BISAC: FICTION / Short Stories

Cover and interior book design by Wendy Saade
Cover photograph by Bill Eastabrook


Published by Morgan Road

www.morganroad.com

# Table of Contents

*For Frank*

# Farewell True Love

The bittersweet lyrics of popular music warp the promise of true love like carnival funhouse mirrors. Every musical genre, from classic torch songs to top 40 hits and country standards, traffics in the co-dependent cultural feedback loop of longing and completion. In the rarified air of a healthy relationship, the wise do not clown around. They are quick to recognize the inevitable, accept that choices have been made and move on with their lives.

My trip to New York had been planned for months. So had her wedding. "In June," Lauren said. "I'm going to be married in June." And I knew I had to see her one last time.

A week before the trip I wondered what old school wisdom John Wayne would offer. Like a scene in the officer's club from *The Fighting Leathernecks*, I imagined the icon of male independence with his elbow planted on the bar. The bartender brought a round of Irish whiskey. Wayne lit a Lucky Strike and spit tobacco on the floor.

"Ah hell, kid. Love can destroy a man in the worst way," he said. "If it's your time a bullet will kill you quick. With a woman it can take years." We toasted the Marine Corps. He downed the drink. "It doesn't matter what I say. You're going to see her anyway."

I made the call. Lauren's voice filled with cheer.

"I will be married on the twenty-seventh," she said. "Can you believe it?"

"You deserve happiness," I said. "More than anyone I know."

Lauren paused. "I wish things were different. I wish you could be there."

"I wouldn't want Jeffrey to be jealous."

"He's not that way. You'd like him."

I did not want to know Jeffrey. "Of course. You're right."

"Okay," she said. "I'll see you next week."

Lauren knew how things were supposed to be. Unlike before, we would only have lunch and I was to call her at work. Although we had exchanged cards and spoken on the phone, we had not seen each other for two years, not since she met Jeffrey. The last time was over a muggy July heat wave weekend in 1987. I'd flown into Washington D.C. and spent the day surveying a 400-unit apartment complex in Silver Spring, Maryland. Plagued with vacancies, the property needed a makeover, a new identity and direction. The heat and humidity soaked my shirt as I crossed the grounds taking reference photographs. I took a cab to the rail station, changed clothes and caught the 6:15 train to New York.

When the train reached Baltimore I moved to the club car. Drinkers celebrated the Dow Jones Industrial Average atop 2,500. I nursed a beer and lost myself in the fading light, stared at the rush of graffiti-scarred bridges and urban row houses with children playing in streets that dead end into the railway. The train plunged into a tunnel, exited to tangerine-tinted twilight through a stand of trees then across a bridge over water like glass. Lifeless sails clung to masts as sailboats motored toward their moorings.

I thought about Lauren and a restless night years before traveling with her on the Amalfi Coast. Our room overlooked the Mediterranean. A breeze slipped through the French doors bearing the fragrance of hillside lemon orchards. Lauren slept with the bedclothes pulled tight. On the horizon a glow drew me onto the balcony. The full moon rose, a surreal golden reflection played across the water. A solitary tanker ship passed through the moonlight and was gone.

The train rocked me back into the present. I returned to the passenger car. A woman in a gingham dress held a baby against her shoulder and read an article about the reunification of Germany. The infant gazed with clear blue eyes, smiled and drooled animal crackers down the back of the mother's dress. When we neared New York, the train stopped then lurched forward through the tunnel into Manhattan.

Outside Penn Station exhaust fumes tinted the clammy night air. I hailed a cab. Weariness yielded to anticipation as I reached Sixty-Second Street. A vendor sold flowers in front of Lauren's building. I considered buying roses, but that would be too much. The doorman announced my arrival then escorted me to the elevator. I hesitated at her apartment door then tapped softly.

Lauren's face flushed with excitement. I must have looked much the same.

"Welcome to New York," she said.

I dropped my bag. We embraced and for a moment the distance between us seemed to vanish. Her studio apartment featured a blue love seat, a drop-leaf table, two chairs, an antique dresser and a trundle bed. A print of Picasso's *Girl Before a Mirror* hung on the wall.

"What do you think?"

"You look great," I said. "You've cut your hair."

"What about my apartment?"

"Elegant. Efficient."

Her lips curled in dissent. "I've worked hard for this."

"This is an excellent space for no other reason than we are in it." I touched her face. "I've missed you."

"And I've missed you." She pulled away. "But let's not dwell on the past. That will only make us sad."

"You're right. Let's make the most of our time."

We settled in an English pub a few blocks away and ordered pints of ale, a departure from her perpetual weight loss program. After the second round we drifted back to how we met in Dallas on my thirtieth birthday. Friends threw a party. Lauren provided the big surprise. When we were introduced everything in the room faded into the background like props in a Broadway play. Lauren's brown eyes sparkled. I listened intently as she spoke about Monet's years at Giverny and the inherent beauty of a world slightly out of focus. She shared how much she loved the Beatles and Joan Baez. On that night the winter sky in Texas was clear and cold and filled with a million shining stars.

"The secretaries in the law office usually go out after work," she said. "Our apartments are too small for entertaining. We meet different places."

"Do you and your friends have any luck?"

"Luck? With what?"

"Meeting men."

"Please." She laughed. "Spare me."

Lauren never enjoyed dating. She was either with someone or she wasn't. Her reluctance to become involved kindled my faint hopes. I made a half-hearted attempt to be supportive of her new life.

"You'd think in New York you'd meet some nice men."

She shredded the corner of a cocktail napkin. "The older we get the harder it becomes," she said. "In case you've forgotten, I'm thirty-five."

"Thirty-five? You are ancient. You're the eighth Wonder of the World."

Lauren slid her hand across the table and tugged playfully at the hairs on the back of my hand, an odd form of petting I never discouraged.

"I'm glad you're here," she said.

The ale lifted our spirits. Outside, the evening air had become a Turkish bath house. Traffic moved then stalled. Taxi drivers sounded horns. We held hands and strolled down Sixty-Second Street singing *I Feel Fine* by The Beatles. An elderly couple applauded as we passed. We sang and hummed until we reached the flower vendor in front of her building.

"Daisies are my favorite." She inspected a bouquet. "They are unpretentious and sunny, don't you think?"

"Of course. You should have them."

That evening was not like before when nothing would have separated us, when we couldn't wait to be alone and time always worked against us. But that night in New York we slept side by side on her trundle beds. I watched her sleep and recalled the last six months we lived together in Dallas in a spacious apartment near Mocking Bird Lane surrounded by huge oak trees. I remembered the sound of leaves rustling in the summer breeze. On those nights near the end, after we made love, Lauren would whisper, "Where could we go from here?" On those nights near the end I held her knowing, regardless of my answer, that she would move to New York.

The next morning Lauren rose early. I waited in bed until she had dressed. The daisies graced a crystal vase on the windowsill that tossed a rainbow of morning light across the room. Lauren prepared scrambled eggs, English muffins, and orange juice. When we finished our coffee she seemed eager to leave the apartment. We walked eight blocks in the sticky heat to Central Park. Joggers passed. A group of cyclists wiped sweat from their brows. Pigeons rested in the shade. When it's hot people with money leave the city, but we were there climbing on the bronze statue of Alice in Wonderland like a pair of mischievous children. We watched a young couple roll in the grass. They giggled and fondled each other without regard to onlookers.

"Human beings are the only mammals that prefer to copulate in private," I said. "These two are exceptional."

"You're right." Lauren studied their undulations. "They're animals. They probably have fleas after rolling around in that grass."

As we exited the park we stopped beside a pond where people raced model sailboats. We held hands and fell into a familiar silence. "Where could we go from here?" she had asked. In love there are often no clear answers, only a narrow bridge that some are unwilling to cross. Dreams converge in surprising and wonderful ways then veer off in new directions. Our shared silence hung like a ceremonial flag draped in the breathless summer heat. We wandered though the afternoon window-shopping, browsing booksellers and department stores. In a small bistro on Fifty-Ninth we lingered over poached salmon and Chardonnay.

She touched my hand. "It's getting late," she said. "We'd better head back."

A welcome breeze coursed through the busy streets and hurried up the buildings. Silence had consumed too much of the day. Patterned impulses ebbed and flowed, pulled us together and pushed us apart. The instincts for love and survival raced along on a collision course where a cruel destiny prevailed with the resolve of logical choices. We abandon the sanctity of our emotional connection. We chose what was right, what was expected.

Lauren stood in the doorway of her bathroom. "I'm going to take a shower," she said.

"Do you want company?"

She shook her head. "That's probably not a good idea."

"We can turn out the lights."

Lauren stepped toward me. I touched the ribbon that secured her gown. We kissed, her lips searched as if she had forgotten that part of herself I knew so well. For moments we connected, bridged the abyss and lingered, slipping back and forth without thought or reservation. Then, like children waking from a dream, we remembered where we were and how it had been. We held each other through that night, but the refuge of sleep soon yielded to the dull gray light of dawn.

That heat wave weekend was two years ago. Soon afterward Lauren met a good man in Manhattan. "Jogging in the park," she said. "How about that?" When she telephoned and confessed she was in love, I congratulated her.

I bought a new suit for the trip to New York, a double-breasted black virgin wool. The city enjoyed a cool June, the sky clear and blue. I appeared crisp and formal as I entered the café Lauren chose for our luncheon. She jumped up. I kissed her forehead.

"The prospects of marriage agree with you," I said.

She stepped back to show off her trim figure and the clean lines of her yellow silk dress.

"He prefers me thin."

"Good for him," I said.

We ordered a split Cobb salad and iced tea. She nibbled at a piece of crusty sour dough bread and told me how they planned to live and travel and how they hoped to have a child.

"Before, I didn't know if I wanted to be a mother. Now I'm certain. You have to be sure of something that important. Don't you think?"

"You'll make a fine mother."

After a long pause she reached for my hand. "I hope we can always be close," she said. Her eyes filled with tears.

"Does Jeffrey know we're having lunch?"

"I don't think he'd understand." She withdrew her hand. "I don't want to risk hurting his feelings."

Lauren insisted on paying for lunch. We walked side-by-side west on Seventy-Second Street toward the Metropolitan Museum where she planned to meet one of her bridesmaids. The budding leaves on the small trees were lush and green. I felt compelled to pause and touch them, to welcome those buds into this life. But I did not stop. We hurried across Fifth Avenue and climbed the many long steps to the entrance of the museum crowded with people coming and going. Exhibition banners, hanging from the museum facade, unfurled in the gentle breeze. When we reached the top of the steps Lauren began to cry. The tears rolled down powdered cheeks, across her lips and onto the yellow silk dress. We embraced.

"You're my best friend," she said. "I don't want to lose you."

I swallowed hard, held it in. "And you're my best friend."

"I love you," she said.

I smelled her hair for the last time. "And I will always love you."

My fingers slipped from her shoulders. I kissed her lips and turned away, every step down to Fifth Avenue deliberate. I walked straight and tall. John Wayne would have been proud. I called a cab, turned and looked up at Lauren in the yellow silk dress with the museum banners floating behind her. She wiped tears from her cheeks and waved. I waved too, but it was more of a salute. I jumped into the cab, headed south on Fifth Avenue and didn't look back until it was too late.

# The Myth of the California Girl

The late afternoon sun reflected off a building across Sunset Boulevard beside a billboard that presented *The Accidental Tourist* for best picture of 1988. Santa Anna winds swept dry heat down from the high desert as stragglers crowded into the back of Millie's, a small café popular with poets and East Hollywood types who wear leather year round. The young Italian woman possessed a sleek figure, thick black hair and a face that may have once held the promise of beauty. The weathered biker jacket draped on her chair reeked of cigarettes. She stepped forward and pressed her lips against the microphone.

"I was born to straddle a Harley Davidson." Her voice trembled as she recited three short poems about her latest lovers, married men with motorcycles. Her eyes welled with tears as she exposed the desire for love and her poor choices. Through the partition a middle-aged woman in a white tank top with a rose tattoo on her right shoulder cooked hamburgers. Sweat threatened to streak from her temples as she labored over the grill. Customers at the counter sipped coffee and waited.

A burst of applause pulled me back into the reading. The Italian woman returned to the seat next to mine. The poetry paused. She went outside to smoke. I opened the *L.A. Reader* and found a personal ad that danced off the page: SWF, California girl, 26, seeks independent man for intellectual, artistic and athletic pursuits possibly even a relationship. Photo and provocative inquiry preferred. #131.

Neither the Italian woman nor the cook could have written that ad. I suspected they were Jersey Shore exiles, not the mythical West Coast being I had hoped to find. For two years I had nurtured this wild fantasy about the ultimate woman: the California girl, kind and enlightened, wild hair blowing in the breeze.

Surfer Bob and I had discussed the California girl mystique on the beach at San Clemente the summer before. Surfer Bob went off on this metaphorical long board riff about women, the harmony of nature and surfing; his speech laced with sordid innuendos about swells, making waves, cutting back, riding the tip, and shooting the tube. It was apparent from my observations that surfing was best done alone. The girls at the beach are either young or very young. Surfers wear UV-coated sunglasses so when beach girls smile they aren't blinded by the glare from their braces. I preferred mature woman with life experience and a sense of humor. I would see if that was possible with a twenty-six-year-old. A dozen years age difference shouldn't be too much to overcome.

I left Millie's and considered the optimum approach as I drove up into Hollywood. When I closed my apartment door the neighbor's television blared the opening theme for *The Wonder Years*. A wave of inspiration crested and the words came.

IN RESPONSE TO YOUR PERSONAL AD
I don't know you, but I am certain you have dreams.
I have a few, yet to come true.
Dreams about children playing along the stretching
sunny beach we walk together.
The dreams of youth are strong and bright and
unburdened by broken promises.
They blow like breezes off the ocean, full of joy and life.
The dreams of youth are strong.
I have a few, yet to come true. Of their beauty I am
certain.
Perhaps one of them is you.

I included my telephone number and a photograph tak-
en on a Mammoth Mountain ski trip. One evening a week
later my telephone rang.

"Why is pain the breeding ground for inspiration?" Her
raspy voice sounded like a jazz singer after an all night jam.

"Hello," I said.

"Why is love a resignation? Do you have the answer?"

"Yes," I said. "A man without possessions rarely tips the
bellman."

A muffled laugh, the clinking of ice cubes turning in a
glass.

"Very good. My name is Felicia, from the personals."

Our conversation began like warm-up volleys in a Los
Angeles Open tennis match. We discussed pollution in Santa
Monica Bay, the tragedy of Tiananmen Square, and the local
poetry scene; how she was born in California and wanted to
open a restaurant.

"Felicia's Evangelical Deli," she said. "We don't speak in tongue, we slice them. What do you think?"

"Provocative," I said. "Memorable."

"I'm not sure about the name. Or where I'll find the money. Right now I'm waiting tables, but it's healthy to have dreams."

"Dreams reflect the spirit of our humanity."

"I loved your poem," she said. "It was a bit saccharin, but optimistic."

"It was honest," I said. "So, when can we meet?"

"Thursday night, ten-thirty, Club Lingerie."

"How will I know you?"

"It's sweet that you haven't asked what I look like. I have your picture. Be on the dance floor. I'll find you."

I hung up, felt excited and somewhat foolish. What kind of person would place a personal ad? And what kind would answer?

Club Lingerie's pink neon sign flickered in the warm night air. The line was short and attended by a large woman with green hair wearing a Comedy Relief II T-shirt. A leashed rat perched on her left shoulder. She took a long drag off a Marlboro and made my change.

"Nice rat," I said.

She ignored me. Inside, through the smoke and semi-darkness, the band Screaming Pygmies played their cover version of *Stairway to Heaven*. Two guys at the bar began shoving each other. I made my way to the edge of the dance floor filled with couples and women dancing alone. One dancer whirled like a Sufi dervish, falling deep into her experience with head thrown back and eyes shut. The zippers on her black leather jacket reflected light from the disco ball.

The song ended. The dervish woman steadied herself. Once grounded, she moved like mercury through the crowd, took my hand and led me to the bar.

"Truth smells like rain," she said. "And it never rains in Southern California. Does it?"

"Not lately."

I loved her voice, her robin blue eyes, and the confidence in her squared jaw. In an instant I knew we would never be lovers. She was too free, too young, looking for Prince Charming in a leather jacket. We had tequila shots then danced for an hour. After midnight we walked to her old Chevy Nova. The car door creaked and moaned. She began to sob.

"Fifty men and two women responded to my ad," she said. "I'm sad because their letters were so lonely or confused. But I'm happy that we met."

"Me, too."

"Now you know a real California girl. I have even surfed at Huntington Beach." She wiped a tear with the sleeve of her jacket.

"Be careful with those zippers," I said. "Good luck finding what you want."

Her car clattered to a start. She waved goodbye. The night became still and quiet. I stood on the empty sidewalk for a long time, thought about a woman my age back in Texas and the way the air smells in Hill Country after a spring rain.

# Prudence in Hollywood

I went to the gynecologist last week, which isn't all that unusual except I'm a man. Prudence insisted I go. I love women, but I don't understand them. And I certainly don't understand what about me is so attractive to dysfunctional females. Of course, I keep going out with them, which says a lot about me.

I met Prudence at a Hollywood Singles lecture on "Honorable Sexuality." We were the only two people who showed, so naturally we talked. Bright and beautiful with long auburn hair Prudence's blue-green eyes seemed to change color according to her mood. Quick to smile, her lips were full and inviting. Prudence, however, lived in Hollywood and my experience has been that Hollywood women are like schnauzers on speed. They don't know where they are going, but they go as fast as they can.

On our second date, with this incredibly dramatic, sexy voice, Prudence asked me to take her home. When we pulled onto Orange Avenue a street sign had been altered by vandals to read: SLOW ADULT CHILDREN PLAYING. I thought the sign quite funny, but Prudence did not laugh. I parked and we walked to her front porch. Most people have a doormat that says: "Welcome." Hers read, "We'll see about that." I guess

I was lucky, because she let me in.

Decorated in early Hollywood struggle her bungalow featured a vintage lava lamp that had belonged to her mother, a worn star-splattered slipcover on her couch and on the wall, flooded by track lights, hung photographs of tinsel town's most notorious martyrs: Elvis Presley, Marilyn Monroe and James Dean.

Prudence asked me to sit and went to release Chopper, her cross-eyed cocker spaniel, from the bathroom. Chopper raced around the apartment, bounced into my lap and started licking me.

"Hey," I said. "Your dog's face is all wet."

"Sorry." Prudence shouted from the bathroom. "I didn't hear you."

"Your dog's all wet."

"Chopper likes to drink from the toilet," Prudence said. "But what can you expect, astrologically, she's a water sign."

Prudence served herbal tea. She dimmed the lights, kicked off her shoes and snuggled into the star-covered couch. Her black v-neck sweater slipped off one shoulder. She cradled her cup and began the conversation.

"When you lick an envelope, do you ever think of Mr. Ed?" She noted my blank expression. "You know, the talking horse."

"No," I said. "I've never had that thought."

She moved closer. Body heat activated her perfume, she smelled like a cosmetics department on Christmas Eve. Her voice became deeper, more provocative. "I love being a woman," she shared. "I even love my period. It's like once a month my body becomes a self-cleaning oven."

"Well," I said. "That's a marketable concept if I've ever heard one."

She leaned toward me until I could feel her breath in my ear then whispered, "Would it turn you on if I talked baby talk?"

I looked into her sparkling eyes. Beads of sweat rolled between my shoulder blades. I gasped for breath and said, "Yes, but only if you promise to change my diapers."

Prudence laughed. "I think I like you." She kissed my cheek, closed her eyes and leaned her head against the couch. I pressed my lips to her neck and could feel the blood pulsing. I kissed her neck. She moaned and shifted her weight against me. We kissed. Soft, sweet kisses quickly escalated into a perverse, addictive, slobbering exchange. The world began to spin faster and faster. Our hands began to roam. And that is when Chopper jumped on the couch and buried her freshly soaked snout in my crotch.

I screamed. Prudence burst out laughing. She scolded her dog, brought a towel and sat beside me while I mopped my trousers.

"I really like you." She lowered her voice and fondled my ear. "And I'd like for us to get closer."

I stopped moping my trousers long enough to nod agreement.

"But there's a little problem." She purred and arched her shoulders, pushing her breasts toward my face. "You see, I haven't made love with a man in over a year."

I tried to act unaffected, but that was hopeless. My eyes widened and my palms began to sweat. "I understand," I said. "It's been a long time for me, too."

Prudence placed her hand on my knee and explained if our relationship was going to progress past kissing on the couch, I had to see her doctor.

I sat up and shook my head. "You want me to see your shrink?"

"No, silly. My gynecologist. I want to make sure we're safe. I know how naughty boys can be."

It was a reasonable request that made me feel I could trust Prudence not to stab me in my sleep if I spent the night. She was bright, a great kisser and about as sane as a Hollywood woman can be. This wasn't sheer lust. I knew in a weird sort of way that I truly cared for her. I thought Prudence worthy of the investment and agreed to see her doctor.

There were nine women in the waiting room of the Hollywood Hills OB-GYN. They all looked at me, crossed their legs and turned their heads like part of some synchronized feminist drill team. I did not feel welcome. After announcing my arrival I sat in the corner, buried my face in a six-month-old copy of *New Women* magazine and hoped the waiting room women would appreciate my attempt. Fortunately, I had the next appointment.

I was called into an office and introduced to Dr. Gertrude, a large German woman with a serious demeanor and noticeable absence of facial hair. With clipboard in hand she crossed her arms and inquired, "So, you want to have intercourse with Prudence?"

"Well," I said. "I'm considering it."

Dr. Gertrude showed me into the examination room. I stopped in disbelief. There, under the brightest lights imaginable, sat the throne of humiliation.

"Do I have to put my feet in the stirrups?"

"That won't be necessary," she said. "You are quite accessible." Dr. Gertrude swung the stirrups out of the way, instructed me to remove my pants, lie down and relax.

When a strange woman wearing laytex gloves examines you with a magnifying glass relaxation is virtually impossible. Dr. Gertrude proved very efficient, so I didn't have to relax for long. She asked about my sexual history, took a blood test and, without ceremony, snapped off her gloves and told me I'd have the results in two days. I pulled on my pants, paid the $150 fee and waved a fond farewell to the waiting room women.

We agreed not to see each other until I had the test results. Those forty-eight hours were difficult. Of course, I passed with flying colors, called Prudence and told her I was on my way. It was late afternoon, birds were singing and I was in the mood for wild romance. I drove to Orange Avenue with lustful, Technicolor images of Hoover dam bursting in my brain.

Prudence greeted me fresh from the shower, a short silk robe clinging to her body, but her mood appeared dark. She locked Chopper in the bathroom. We sat on the couch, I shared the good news, but her expression did not change. She held my hand.

"What's wrong?" I asked. "I thought you'd be excited."

"I don't know how to say this."

"I've been to your gynecologist. You can tell me anything."

"It's difficult, because I'm certain I really like you." Prudence squared her shoulders. "But, I've changed my mind."

My eyes crossed. "What?"

"I just have a hard time, you know, mixing sex and love."

"So," I pleaded. "Can you hate me until we get better acquainted?"

"I want to get married and have children."

"That's a great idea. Why don't we work on our technique?" I begged. "Just consider me a vibrator who listens."

She laughed a hollow laugh. "You're sweet," she said. "But I can't explain. This is the way things are for me with men."

She wouldn't budge, no tears, nothing. We held hands and stared at the undulating green ooze convulsing in her mother's lava lamp. There would be no biological breakthrough. We sat on her star-splattered couch and shared an awkward silence that meandered around the frayed edges of our misunderstanding, but we shared the silence and that was a good start.

"Do you want to talk about it?" I asked.

"About what," she said. "Love or sex?"

"Both. Why don't you talk about both?"

It had been dark for over an hour. Prudence turned on a light, retreated to the kitchen and returned with bagels, cream cheese and a Diet Pepsi. Prudence bit into her bagel and chewed with a tiny bit of cream cheese smeared on the end of her nose.

"You can't discuss loneliness on an empty stomach," she said.

We ate and talked about almost everything, except love and sex.

"So, what about it?" I asked.

She dipped a finger into the cream cheese and licked.

"You don't give up do you?"

I shook my head.

"Okay. It's like this, if I sleep with a man I'm not seriously interested in, he always comes back wanting more and it takes a lot of effort to get rid of him." She shifted her weight and looked at the floor. "If I sleep with a man I actually care about, and I tell him I care, he runs the other way. It's a cruel, childish game."

"But it doesn't have to be that way," I said. "Not all men are like that."

I stroked her back. She caressed my knee. We hugged a good, long hug. I closed my eyes and smelled the heavy fragrance of her dusting powder. I think it was Tabu. When I opened my eyes all I could see was the glowing green ooze of the lava lamp. It had grown late. Prudence insisted I spend the night on her couch. She brought a pillow and blanket. When we kissed good night she purred like a cat.

At one a.m. I awoke to muffled sounds coming from the other room. "YUMMMMM, YUMMMMM, YUMMMMM." I stumbled into the kitchen and found Prudence at the table face down in a bucket of double Dutch chocolate ice cream. I rubbed my eyes.

"My God," I muttered. "You need help. Where are the spoons?"

"I didn't intend to wake you," she said. "I just had this incredible craving."

"I know exactly how that feels."

I pulled a tablespoon and a bowl from the dish rack. Chopper sat on the floor beneath Prudence, wagging her stubby tail and drooling. I scooped some ice cream from the bucket and motioned to the dog. "Is this okay?"

Prudence nodded approval. I sat the bowl on the floor and Chopper went to work. Prudence rubbed Chopper's back with long, tender strokes, looked at me and smiled. Her teeth showed white against the dark chocolate smudged across her lips, chin and cheeks. She scooted on the breakfast bench.

"Chopper's usually afraid of men." Prudence smiled and patted the seat. "But I think she likes you."

"Well." I sat on the bench close to her. "I know I like you."

I gazed into the dreamy invitation of her eyes. She ran her tongue along the puffy fullness of her upper lip and whispered, "Kiss me."

We kissed slowly and deeply. And we laughed. We stuck our fingers in the bucket and smeared ice cream across our lips and faces and licked each other from nose to chin and from ear to ear. Our lips and tongues explored the depths of the ice cream fantasy. We embraced and began our glorious journey together, moaning in unison, "YUM, YUM, YUM."

More than passion mixed with double Dutch chocolate, this was the ultimate kiss, hot enough to melt a hundred valentines and just as sweet. Our passion melted into a celebration of trust and understanding. A celebration of love that began with an innocent snack in the kitchen and ended with a fabulous feast in the bedroom, a feast of recognition, discovery and joy. A feast of laughter in which I could not think of anything except satisfying Prudence and my thoughts were rewarded in the most wonderful, sticky ways.

# Kind of Blue

Her eyes are black like the La Brea Tar Pits on a moonless night. Only the brave or imbalanced venture near. She dances from the darkness, shields her lavender-scented candle. The flame illuminates the curves beneath her satin robe, a shimmering cobalt blue. She traces a delicate path along her neck. "Kiss me here," she says. "Softly with your lips parted." There is no retreat. Our breath quickens. The room expands. Through the evening our disordered love unfolds. Everything rises and falls like summer rain upon the sea.

Selena and I had navigated the boundaries of love and desire and friendship. We nurtured our fantasies like crazed children in a birthday bounce house. But in life there could not be a child between us. Nature has laws and thresholds and the march of time. Lovers eventually reach the juncture where the deepening lines in her mirror may no longer be ignored. Nature gave women the freedom to choose.

Months had passed since the fateful Halloween costume party in West Covina. Selena designed a Jack O' Lantern for her nine-year-old niece Carmen. In Day of the Dead fashion, an artful nod to the pagan Aztec festival, Selena painted the pumpkin white and carved blank eyes and elongated teeth.

As the party unwound we took a photograph on the porch: the Jack O' Lantern, Selena, Carmen and me dressed, respectively, as Wonder Woman, Tinker Bell and Indiana Jones. After the photograph Selena handed me her creation. I stumbled and the pumpkin smashed against the sidewalk. Little Carmen, to her credit, did not cry. Quietly and with Tinker Bell flair, Carmen sprinkled pixie dust on the orange-fruited remains. My position was defenseless as I scooped pumpkin chunks into a trash bag understanding there would be consequences. A pleasant autumn evening turned suddenly cold. I covered Selena's bare shoulders with my leather jacket. She did not protest or speak until we reached the door of her building.

"You better go," she said.

I accepted that costumed encounter had been our last. So, months later, Selena's phone call was a surprise. In the background a siren screamed as an ambulance passed through her Fairfax neighborhood.

"Hey," she said. "You forgot your jacket."

"That was four months ago."

"Why don't you come for lunch on Saturday?"

"Just like that?"

"Sure," she said. "Exactly like that. We'll eat Chinese, like old times. I have a story to tell."

On Saturday I drove east on the Santa Monica Freeway listening to Miles Davis' *Kind of Blue*, the album I played the first night Selena came to my apartment. I was encouraged that she recognized the music and thought about how the satin robe became part of our ritual. How we fumbled along reaching for something that remained just beyond our grasp.

"Slow," she said. "Make it go slow." The tide rose, our toes curled and cramped. The robe cast aside. We moaned and groaned. The upstairs neighbor often stomped her feet in protest. "She's jealous," Selena said.

Selena struck a pose in her doorway wearing faded jeans and a festive red cashmere sweater. Her jet-black hair shined like silk against her skin.

"Hello stranger."

"Hello yourself."

Selena offered her hand, showed me several paintings, surreal yellow sunflowers rising from the canvas with layers of modeling paste and acrylic paint.

"New technique?"

"A tribute really." Her voice sounded confident. "You know how much I love Van Gogh."

We sat on her zebra pattern sofa. The half circle coffee table was painted like a slice of seedless watermelon. I admired her paintings and searched for something to say.

"You've been busy."

"Referring to my work?"

"Everything. The paintings are excellent, of course, but it's you. You seem almost happy."

"I think that I am happy. It's been an awkward yet productive time."

She placed a bare foot on the coffee table and extended it toward me. I reached for the arch of her sole.

"I'd rather you didn't."

"Forgive me. I wasn't…"

"It's okay." Selena smiled. "No problem."

I stared at the ceiling. "How about your friend upstairs,

thunder foot?"

Selena laughed. "I have not given her cause to protest."

She excused herself. My mind wandered back to Halloween and Wonder Woman, Selena wearing my leather jacket. I imagined forgiveness, a twist of fate, Selena wearing the robe, intent on having her way.

"I crave Chinese food." Selena carried my leather jacket and a small black purse. "And drinking sake."

At Chopstix on Melrose Avenue we took a patio table shaded from the sun. The waitress brought sake. Selena finished her cup in two drinks. Never shy about drinking, she drank to relax or fortify her resolve. Even in a mild state of intoxication she was capable of anything. Selena planted her fingernails into my forearm.

"Why haven't you called?"

I refused to flinch. "Don't you remember?" I formed my words carefully. "You said you wanted to take a break."

"Over smashing my pumpkin?"

"It was before that happened."

She released her grip. "I did say that. But not forever."

"That's good." I took a breath and sipped sake. "Because I can't stop thinking about you."

"That's such trash. You didn't even call on my birthday."

"You asked me not to call. I sent a Christmas card."

"You send everyone a Christmas card."

"But it's true." I knew better, that a man should be cautious with forthcomings. "I've thought about you every day."

Selena poured sake. We ate spring rolls, steamed vegetables and brown rice. She wiped a spot of plum sauce from her chin, filled our sake cups and reclined in her chair.

"I had a couple of disaster dates," she said. "Then I said 'to hell with love' and focused on securing new commissions. Fortunately, the work has come."

Her condemnation of dating unsettled me. "Popular culture programs society to a set of fictionalized romantic ideals," I said. "They're tragic, every one of them. Cinderella and 'happily ever after' is just as deranged as Romeo and Juliet. In *The Los Angeles Times* I read about this 71-year-old woman arrested after she allegedly doused her husband with rubbing alcohol and set him on fire. Why? Because he ate a chocolate Easter bunny she had saved for herself."

Selena lifted her drink. "A guy that age should know better than to touch a woman's chocolate."

"They had been married thirty years. She burned him while he was sleeping in their bed."

"The punishment fits the crime."

The waitress brought our check, two fortune cookies and a carryout box with leftover vegetables.

"Pardon me," Selena said. "I have to go floss my teeth. I know how much you hate to watch."

"I love watching you floss, just not in the middle of a restaurant."

My fortune cookie read: "Be sensitive to the feelings of others." I watched the traffic on Melrose until Selena returned, her eyes hidden behind Ray-Ban shades.

"The day is beautiful," she said. "Let's go to the beach."

"The beach? I thought you were going to an art show."

"It's a party and not until much later. Come on, let's go."

I navigated through the traffic on I-10, west through the tunnel and north onto Pacific Coast Highway. We cracked the windows to welcome the cool ocean air. Jim Morrison sang *Roadhouse Blues* as we passed between the cliffs of Palisades Park and the sparkling Pacific. I recalled a dream where I am a seabird flying across the water. Beyond the breaking waves the ocean is clear and schools of baitfish swim like morphed clouds. Dolphins chase the fish skyward where they are easy prey.

I parked at Topanga State Beach. Selena rolled the cuffs of her jeans, removed her bondage sandals and spread her freshly painted red toenails. I carried her over a stretch of jagged rocks. We walked the shoreline. Surf churned against the scattered stones. Seagulls sailed. Selena drew a broken shell from the wet sand and shielded her face from the sun. The sky was unusually clear. We could see all the way to Catalina Island.

"I've made a lot of progress this last year." Selena raised her voice above the waves. "I went back into therapy. I've painted every day. I feel whole now, not a part of anything else, but just me."

The cool air took the edge off the sake. I tossed a stone into the surf and watched the swells. It was the time of day the ocean turned from blue to gray.

"I was going along fine." She turned the broken shell in her hands. "In February I went to this new club on Highland with my friend Beth. You know Beth. Well, we got a little drunk and started dancing. When Prince's *Little Red Corvette* ended we hugged then it happened. I can't explain why, except she kissed me and it was really nice and then I kissed her. Right there, in front of about a hundred people, we made out like crazy."

My shoulders sank. "We drove all the way out here so you could share the details of making out with Beth?"

"No, you're my friend. You know I like men. Kissing Beth was spontaneous like tasting dip samples at Costco. It happened then stopped. It's not like I went home with her or anything."

"And the point of the story?"

"With guys there always has to be a point."

"Not necessarily," I said. "But I bet you have one."

"That night, after we kissed, practically every other guy in the club became a mental patient. A dozen men and two women hit on us. Beth told them to get lost, but this one guy was persistent. His name is Caeṣar. He made me laugh and seemed really sweet. We started talking. We've been going out, taking our time. I wanted you to know that I really like Caesar. He wants to live on a ranch and raise horses. Pretty wild, huh?"

I tossed a stone into the waves and turned away from the ocean. The Santa Monica Mountains loomed, slopes blackened from wildfires. We walked back down the beach. When we reached the jagged rocks I carried her again. She wrapped her legs around me and squeezed.

"It's good to see you."

She wiggled her painted toes. I let her down.

"I hope everything works out," I said.

She brushed the hair from her face and glanced toward the ocean.

"I think we usually get what we want. Don't you?"

I didn't answer. The sun surrendered to the sea. We headed south on Pacific Coast Highway through the tunnel and east onto the Santa Monica Freeway. Street lamps flickered to life when I turned off Fairfax Avenue. Selena grabbed her Chinese leftovers and smiled sweetly.

"Let's stay in touch. Promise?"

I nodded and watched her walk away. My leather jacket carried the scent of lavender and Selena. I drove home grateful my friend had found steady ground. In my dreams I won't see her with Beth or an urban cowboy named Caesar. In my dreams Selena will always be my lover, an apparition with whom I shared many joyful moments. Her eyes are black as coal. They twinkle with anticipation. The satin robe wrapped tight like a funeral shroud. "My sweet," she whispers. I close my eyes as if entombed and all I see is blue.

# *Lover Boy*

The days of a recovering love junkie are filled with reso-
lution. In the late 90s, I lived at the beach in Southern
California, an endless summer scene where surfers
feast on fish tacos and tourists troll the Esplanade at Sunset. The turning point was the morning I awoke face-down
in Claudette's shag carpet wearing Chinese handcuffs—the
joke ones that tighten on your fingers when pulled apart—
with a stabbing pain in my back and an African gray parrot
screaming, "Wake up, Lover Boy. Wake up."

I resolved to go clean, to stop worshipping the moon, but
the gravitational pull of the sacred feminine will not release
me. For the women I have known Mercury, the planet that
rules communications, always seemed to be in retrograde.
Claudette was no exception. Her sultry French accent magnified the intensity of everything. In the wake of her confession I experienced acute withdrawal symptoms. Depression
reigned. I was haunted by nightmares of Claudette burning
wedding photographs in a flaming pit. At 3 a.m. every morning I lurched like a zombie from the grave, my tongue dry as
driftwood.

Normally I would not seek the advice of a psychic. A double vodka martini is easier to swallow. My neighbor friend

Maui brought miso soup and a California roll. "I know how you feel," she said. "Sometimes I can't sleep, even when I am happy. You need to eat and go to see the astrologer. She will help." Maui insisted my mental woes would benefit from a reading. I'm loyal to my therapist, but wanted a second opinion.

Shirley the psychic rattled around her kitchen like a twenty-year-old taxi. I waited in the parlor, my olfactory senses challenged by a blend of freshly brewed chamomile, burned sage and analgesic balm. Primitive masks adorned the walls. Dusty books littered the floor. An air conditioner hummed in a living room window framed by thick velvet drapes. A weathered sign by the door read: THIS WAY TO THE BEACH.

The beaded glass curtain parted. Shirley clutched a Lord of the Rings stein and settled across the table. A crooked finger scanned the chart. Here eyes closed.

"Spirits guide us night and day," she chanted. "Give us wisdom, show us the way." Her eyes opened. She sipped from the mug. "You are an old soul. As a child you were solemn and responsible. With age you've become more playful and spontaneous. This progress is healthy."

Despite the dull pain pulsating across my back I employed my best poker face, the one I use in vain at Commerce Casino.

"Your past looms like the shadow of a great mountain. You must release the past. This is the only way the patterns of your life will be changed. Mars has a heavy influence. You are passionate and sometimes warlike. You are impatient."

On the bookcase an antique clock clicked and clacked.

Shirley marshaled on like a dating columnist for *Cosmopolitan* magazine.

"You must learn to love yourself." She rapped a gnarled knuckle against the table. "Relationships flow from an open heart. Beware of the one you love. I see a cardinal cross. She is passionate, but she will never be content. The prospect of satisfying her is an exciting challenge for an old soul like you because, in your heart, you know that this is impossible."

The clock chimed. Shirley pressed an index finger to her lips. I shelled out fifty dollars.

"What now?"

"Confide in a close friend." She folded the bills. "Resist your urges."

I went to see Doctor No, my psychotherapist and hired friend. Her actual name is Marilyn Nolander, PhD. At our first meeting, a few years ago, I made the mistake of suggesting I was self-actualized. Doctor No spent three sessions breaking down how that could not be. She's right. I was probably beyond help, but I liked her style. She would be attractive if she smiled. Her seriousness was a shield against suffering.

"You don't remember what happened?"

Doctor No adjusted her reading glasses and scribbled on a yellow legal pad.

"It was weird," I said. "We were drinking pinot noir. Claudette had been distant since the Fourth of July. That's when she began kissing me on the cheek like I was her brother.'"

"You blacked out drinking wine?"

"We killed the bottle in twenty minutes. She starts in with 'I'm not a good girlfriend.' I had an emotional meltdown. I couldn't breathe. Fade to black. I wake up in pain, her parrot mocking me at decibel eleven."

I didn't want to tell Doctor No about Claudette's confession or how I cried like a baby, and that I smoked a flavored strain of weed prescribed for hospice patients called Knock Out Punch.

"It's a haze," I said. "But I'm not an alcoholic."

"You have to accept there's an issue." Doctor No cleared her throat. "Alcoholics and addicts lie. That's what they do. Remember your parents."

I stared at the pile of designer pillows on the floor, imagined Claudette's parted lips and the subtle gap in her teeth. The words tumbled off my tongue. "I'm addicted to love," I said. "The desire for a deep and meaningful physical connection."

Doctor No presented a plastic bat and gestured toward the pillows.

"Have a go," she said. "Unfulfilled desire is the source of your pain. Vent your sadness and disappointment. It's okay to scream."

The suggestion of violence made me nauseous. "I thought women appreciated men who are emotionally available."

"Emotionally balanced," she said. "And, in your present state, you are not."

Doctor No struck a nerve, but I didn't flinch. "I'm not into primal screaming. I'll hit the beach. I'll run sprints in the sand."

"We're out of time. What are your resolutions?"

"Besides avoiding Claudette?"

"Yes, leave that alone. What else?"

I thought about it, but not too long. "Avoid happy hour,

codependents anonymous meetings, karaoke, and the organic produce section at Whole Foods Market."

"You are the source of your emotional pain and your healing." Doctor No removed her reading glasses. The eye contact sobered me. "Come in next week ready to share what really happened with Claudette."

Our affair began innocently enough. I was browsing through Henry Miller's *Crazy Cock* in the Either/Or Bookstore on Pier Avenue. Claudette approached looking fresh and out of place in the funky bohemian bookstore named after Swedish philosopher Soren Kirkegaard's first book. French woman are often conflicted French film clichés: resonant with foreboding darkness and overthinking, sexual innuendo and class envy. I could see it coming, but have a weakness for accents and short blond hair. She wore fashionably tight jeans, a classic black T-shirt and a shocking pink scarf. Her skin was fair and unblemished, rare for beach women or Valley girls, and paired perfectly with peach lipstick. I guessed she was mid-forties, about my age.

"I am looking for *The Prophet*. Do you know it?"

"I read it in college," I said. "But I don't work here."

"That is not the question."

"You'll find it in poetry or philosophy."

"I am busy," she said. "My time is precious."

I escorted her to the poetry section. "You want this one," I said. "With the illustrations."

She opened the book. "Beautiful artwork. Thank you."

"My pleasure." I hesitated. "I'd like to see you."

"You see me now."

"Again. I'd like to see you again," I said. "Let's have coffee."

"I drink wine." She presented a business card: Claudette Simone, Fine Art Photography. "I have a booth at the festival near the pier. Find me."

At the beach summer begins with Memorial Day. Claudette's booth featured intimate wedding photographs and family portraits. Every image commanded attention however glossed by sunlight or celebration. A young couple perused Claudette's wedding book sampler. I thumbed through her iconic Southern California prints: Griffith Observatory, Getty Villa, Muscle Beach, Randy's Donuts, Point Dume, a lonely Joshua tree. The couple made notes on a business card then disappeared into the crowd.

"Excellent photography," I said. "I see why you are busy."

Claudette examined my face like a vice squad detective.

"You have good features."

Three athletic women approached wearing Heal the Bay sun visors.

"I'll let you get back to work."

"Call me," she said. "Let's have a glass of wine."

We met at the Seafood Grotto, an old-school dinner place with an ocean view. It was late. The sunset crowd had cleared. An elderly gentleman played *Unforgettable* on a polished grand piano. We took a window table with a view of nothing but darkness, ordered calamari appetizers and Chardonnay.

Into the second glass of wine Claudette shared how she met her husband at Brooks Institute of Photography in Santa Barbara. A childless marriage lasted fifteen years. Now, she and her older sister Raissa rented a house in Hermosa Beach. Thankfully she made no mention of felonious ex-boyfriends or restraining orders.

Claudette played with a lock of hair. "Would you like if my hair was longer?" Her lips parted to show her incisors, marginally askew. "Or if my teeth were perfect? You American men love women with long hair and straight teeth."

The timbre and tempo of her voice charmed me, but my initial reaction, which I did not share, was, "Are you trying to sell a horse?" In poker terms Claudette's comments are considered "tells," an unconscious disclosure of character traits and predictable behavior. I ignored my instinct for self-preservation when it may have mattered. Instead I lumbered along lost in her eyes, clear and green like ocean pools on the beach side of the breakwater.

"Our looks will fade." I placed an open hand over my chest. The wine spoke through me like I was a vaudeville dummy. "The heart knows what is important."

She grinned and took the last of her wine. I was relieved. Humorless people make poor lovers. They rarely have anything joyful or sacred to share. I walked Claudette to her Volvo station wagon. Waves pounded the beach. We embraced. Our first kiss was tight-lipped and tentative.

"Pardon me," she said. "It's been some time."

"When may I see you again?"

"I will make dinner," she said.

Three evenings later, after Claudette's hearty lamb stew and a bottle of Cabernet, we lost our minds on her memory foam mattress. It happened fast. A surprisingly awkward college flashback encounter led to a raucous conclusion. Long caresses ensued. She reciprocated, stroked my head as a hunter would a golden retriever bearing freshly killed pheasants. I drifted toward sleep.

Claudette kissed my shoulder. "Wake up Lover Boy," she whispered.

She donned a dressing gown, excused herself and returned with a leaded crystal plate of strawberries and whipped dairy cream.

I rubbed my eyes. "What?"

"Never question a woman who shares dessert," she said. "Or her bed."

We fed each other berries.

"You are delicious," I said.

That's when I heard an echoed screech, "You are delicious."

"Who's that?"

Claudette smiled. "Lola. My parrot."

She carted the plate into the kitchen and emerged minutes later with the parrot balanced on an index finger. "Lola," she said. "This is my Lover Boy."

"Lover Boy," Lola screeched, clicked her beak and stared me down.

Claudette escorted her pet back to the birdcage. Through the dim light I studied a series of photographs on the far wall. Sensuous nudes explored the subtle curves of a woman's shoulder, hip and buttocks. A large print revealed wide set eyes. In another matted frame the demure model struck a classical pose, turned her face from the camera and covered one breast with a blanket. On cue Claudette returned, her dressing gown unbound.

"These images are remarkable."

"Thank you," she said. "I was young. My ex-husband took

the one of my eyes. The rest are self-portraits."

At the beach June is known as the month of gloom. The marine layer rolls in over night and lingers until the sun burns through. Weeks passed. Claudette busied herself shooting during the day then edited her work in the evening. Every other night we'd go for dinner and a walk, holding hands like teenagers then, as she desired, make love at her place listening to jazz on KCRW. I brought flowers and croissants for her morning coffee. One sleepy Sunday we awoke in my apartment with nothing to do but be together.

Claudette wiggled into my arms. "You are perfect," she said.

"Hardly."

"You are perfect for me."

"Yes," I said. "This feels right."

"Do you go to church?"

Somewhere in the depths of fear an alarm sounded. "Love is my religion," I countered. "You are my church."

Claudette sighed. "Oh, Lover Boy," she said. "When I say that I love you, I love you."

Her affirmation launched my hypothalamus into an ecstatic overdrive. My brain lit up like an arcade pinball machine. Flippers flipped. Lights flashed. Bells rang. I abandoned all rational frontal lobe activity and slid willingly into a pathological puddle of misery disguised as happiness. I had lost my mind and loved it. After she left I found a note on my pillow: My Lover Boy, you will kill me with your sweetness. What a glorious death (la petite mort). Love, Claudette.

Just before sunset on July Fourth I found Claudette's sister Raissa on their balcony fingering a joint the size of a Polish sausage. She lit the monster, inhaled and offered it to me.

"I better pass for now," I said. "Are you coming along?"

"No." She exhaled a thick cumulus cloud of smoke. "I hate people."

"You mean crowds?"

"I hate crowds and people."

As proof of my pathology I blurted, "I love your sister."

Raissa covered a cough with her fist and stared off at the ocean.

"She has a cute figure," she said.

Claudette and I pedaled our beach cruisers along the strand and parked well south of the Redondo Beach pier. That's when my neighbor Maui rolled up on her skates wearing a U.S.A. logo jacket. She smiled, her teeth unmistakably straight and white in the failing light. We hugged in our customary aloha fashion. I introduced Claudette.

"Do you want to watch the fireworks?" I said.

Maui glanced at Claudette. "I better roll along," she said. "I'm meeting some of my girlfriends."

Claudette and I found a spot. I wrapped her in a blanket. Spectators packed the beach and along the Esplanade. At the appointed hour an onslaught of multi-colored rockets rose, flared and exploded over the water. Faces of children and parents glowed with awestruck pyrotechnic reflections. The crowd reverberated with successive groans of approval and applause. Claudette sat stone-faced until the grand finale. We pedaled back to her place. She opened the door and kissed me on the cheek.

"I have an early day tomorrow," she said. "Good night."

"What's this," I said. "What's wrong?"

Claudette's jaw tightened. "Do you love her?"

"Who, Maui?" I said. "She is my friend."

"Do you love your friend?"

"She's from Hawaii. We're friendly. It's absolutely nothing."

Claudette looked away. "I have a wedding in San Francisco. I am busy."

"What does that mean?"

"We will discuss our relationship later."

When I got home I called. No answer. My pinball imagination went on tilt. I attempted sleep while my logical brain recounted Claudette's behavioral tells like a flock of bleating lambs. That weekend I ran wind sprints in the sand. I pulled on my summer wetsuit, swam through beach break waves and floated on my back. A cloudless blue sky granted a measure of comfort as I bobbed along and surrendered to the rhythm of the open sea.

Ten days later Claudette met me at the Spot restaurant for an early dinner. We split an avocado veggie burger.

"How was San Francisco?"

"Cold," she said. "Sunny for the ceremony. Hundreds of photographs."

I exercised restraint. On the walk home I reached for her hand and she accepted.

"What's wrong?"

Claudette waited half a block to answer. "I am not a good girl for you." She dropped her hand. "You deserve someone without my problems."

"Problems? For weeks you said that you loved me. That I was perfect."

"I was drunk," she said. "We drink wine. We make love. We wake up the next day. Life goes on. This is reality."

"We choose our reality."

"I don't argue. I don't like it." At her door she kissed my cheek. "I have work," she said. "We will discuss our relationship another time."

"Please," I said. "It's important. Let's discuss it now."

Claudette relented. "Okay," she said. "Let's have a drink."

I minded my resolutions. The night before my appointment with Doctor No Maui knocked on my door.

"Come on," she said. "Let's go meet Wilson for a drink. You need to cheer up. Having company will be good for you."

We walked to the Brewing Company and ordered Rat Beach amber ale. Wilson made his entrance wearing a hooded Los Angeles Lakers sweatshirt.

Wilson slapped my back. "What's up with the prince of darkness?" he said.

"Am I that transparent?"

"Bro, I read you like a book."

"He broke up with his girlfriend," Maui said. "He's sad."

"You never learn." Wilson ordered a Corona with lime. "Last summer you almost died over that flight attendant. Her eyes didn't match her face. I warned you. She colonized you the first weekend."

"Colonized?" Maui said.

I tasted the amber ale, recalled why I had avoided Wilson. "She left a change of clothing in my apartment," I said. "For when she returned."

Wilson laughed. "Bro, you were bagged and tagged."

"That is so romantic," I said. "You are a regular barroom Romeo."

"Romeo drank the poison, bro. Romance is for suckers." Wilson finished his beer in a gulp. "Don't be such a sap."

Maui stared at Wilson. "You don't believe in love?" she said.

"Suffering is not my thing."

"I'm calling it a night," I said.

"Have another round." Wilson waved to the bartender. "I'm buying."

"One was enough."

People can say whatever they want. I was not raised on fear. My parent's spirits were not moved by hellfire and brimstone. They preferred cocktails. I walked home, the air heavy with cool ocean mist and the thunder of collapsing waves.

Doctor No directed me to the couch. The pile of floor pillows carefully arranged for the next beating. She didn't waste any time.

"So, let's hear it."

I visualized the glass coffee table in Claudette's living room, the San Francisco guidebook, Chinese handcuffs and fortunes cookies. There was a light box, a binder of wedding party proof sheets and film negatives.

"Claudette doesn't like to argue," I said.

Doctor No put her legal pad aside. "Imagine that I am Claudette," she said. "What did you say to her?"

I took a breath and recalled my dreams of the flaming pit. Claudette's photographs curl and melt into the fire.

"You said that you loved me. I could not have loved you

43

more. I was crazy for you, for the sound of your voice and the touch of your hand. Then, without warning, you treat me like a stranger. How is that possible?"

Doctor No cleared her throat. "That intense level of emotional engagement is unsustainable," she said. "All we have in life are moments. They do not last."

"Like chiropractic adjustments," I said. "Or acupuncture." Considering the payment schedule, one would think the purpose of therapy is to make you feel better. That is rarely the case.

Doctor No leaned into her words. "Perhaps the most loving thing Claudette could do was to turn you away."

"That would have been beautiful," I said. "The truth is, after two glasses of wine and repeating how she was not a good girlfriend, she confessed. At the wedding in San Francisco she met a guy."

Doctor No reached for her legal pad.

"A normal reaction is to become upset or scream." I continued, objective and clearheaded. "Part of me wanted to leave, but somehow I couldn't. I just sat there thinking of all the tender moments. Then I imagined her with someone else. And that's when I dropped my face into my hands and began to cry."

"How did Claudette react?"

"She rubbed my back. When I didn't stop crying, she brought a wet cloth for my face, a glass of water and the medical marijuana her sister smokes for chronic pain. Claudette lit the joint. After two hits the room began to wobble. I remember laughing with my thumbs in the Chinese handcuffs. Then I passed out and hit the floor."

Doctor No made notes. "Does Claudette know about your parents?" she said. "About your divorce and other relationships?"

"None of that matters now."

"Love and acceptance are fundamental needs," she said. "That sense of belonging and community defines what it means to be fully human. The betrayal of trust is painful, no different than a broken bone or the death of a loved one. Wounds require time to heal."

"Some wounds never heal," I said. "That is also a possibility."

At 3 a.m. I wandered over to the Esplanade to witness the waning moon vanish beyond a blackened ocean horizon. Alone under a street lamp I considered the recovery of my senses and the raw edges of singlehood. I thought about Claudette's body resting next to mine, the allure of her innocent morning face. In my heart I understood the power of forgiveness and accepted the grace of the great unknown. These reflections triggered a moment of clarity: the reason we are attracted to people is that we do not know them. Some people cannot be known. They are unaware or unwilling to take the risk. And with that I saw her down on the beach, beyond the shadow of a lifeguard tower, my sleepless neighbor friend Maui dancing barefoot in the sand.

# Eating Alone

The Rive Gauche Café sits back from the frenzied crush of Ventura Boulevard, a mature brick and stucco refuge with red tile accents along the roof. Beams of afternoon sunlight pierced the evergreen canopy above the quiet patio dining area. I took a small corner table near the bar. On the opposite wall water pattered into a small pool from the mouth of a concrete lion. Tables with fresh linen and wrought iron chairs stood ready to welcome evening patrons.

The server brought a basket of French bread. "I'm Christine," she said.

"Hello Christine." I didn't open the menu. "I'll have the seafood salad and an iced tea. Unsweetened."

Christine smiled, grateful that I knew what I wanted. Few people do. They struggle with even the smallest things, afraid to make a mistake. The essence of character is often revealed early in life, all the love we know or long to know. The rest is self-expression or conformity. Christine possessed a fearless face. As a child her parents probably read Doctor Seuss stories when they tucked her into bed.

Beneath the evergreens my mind wandered. Years ago, on a snow-shrouded winter's day, I watched my aunt struggle to lift her lifeless legs onto a footstool. She rarely spoke about it, but once shared the pain was like an ice pick chipping into her spine. She sipped coffee, puffed on a cigarette and watched the snow-covered birdbath in her backyard. A family of Cardinals perched on a nearby feeder.

"Those Cardinals come every winter," she said. "Three generations are feeding." The birds fluttered their wings. "Tell me. When did you first realize you were here alone?"

"I don't know."

"Think. This is important."

A wind chime sounded. The Cardinals took flight. I shut my eyes and recalled when, as a small boy, my father and I explored the woods by our home. Slick with autumn leaves, the bank of a stream presented a lurid watercolor scene awash in amber and burnt sienna. He offered his hand and encouraged me to come along. Above us fading light illuminated barren limbs against an empty sky. A cold wind scattered leaves across the stream. I stood alone balanced on a stone. My father paused then headed up the trail. I stared into the shallows with the muddy bottom and leaves floating along. I retrieved a tiny red boat from the mud, washed the plastic, straightened the hull then set it on the water. My father called. His big voice echoed through the woods. I stood alone. The current lifted the boat and for a few brief seconds it floated downstream. The wind came up. The boat tilted and sank. Again, my father called. I scurried up the bank, dead leaves slipped beneath my sneakers.

During the pregnancy my ex-wife was concerned about stretch marks. I would warm oil in my hands then caress her swollen belly. Once, as I lay beside her, she pressed my palm against her stomach. Our son's kick was a willful gesture. I spread my fingers. Did he know his father waited for him to cross over? For his mother the kick was a familiar marvel building as the weeks passed. The thump against my oiled hand served as an affirmation. I hesitated as if balanced on a stone, listened for a familiar voice to echo through the woods.

"I was six years old," I said. "On a hike with my father."

Snow began to fall. My aunt extinguished her cigarette. "Being alone was my earliest memory. I was a toddler. My parents threw a cocktail party. Everyone was drunk. I recall thinking, 'How did I end up in this place with these thoughtless people?'"

Laughter roared from the bar behind me. A group of women celebrated. The waiter brought wine and filled their glasses. The women toasted. In her late thirties, the bride-to-be read a card aloud: *May your love be endless, your children divine.*

"Oh, how sweet," her friends said. "How romantic."

She opened the gift. Her face flushed as she held up a feathered mask, a black negligee and a leather whip.

"Frederick's of Hollywood!" The friends raised their glasses. "How sweet. How romantic."

From Ventura Boulevard a family passed through the patio. The husband carried an infant wrapped in a pink blanket. The wife dragged an empty stroller. Grandparents followed into the dining room. Christine brought my meal. I retreated into the tastes and textures of crabmeat and shrimp, bell peppers, celery and hard-boiled eggs.

The back gate groaned. A well-dressed man in his late sixties appeared with a young olive-skinned woman. "Harry,

I want to be outside," the woman said. "I want to sit outside and have champagne cocktails."

"It will be cold," he said. "There's a draft."

"Please, Harry."

They are seated at a table near the lion-faced fountain. She ordered drinks then draped her arm around the man's shoulders. Sunlight skipped across the tablecloths on the eastside of the patio, my corner now cool in the shade. In the bar, the women drank wine and chatted. A pair of small birds hopped along the brick floor feasting on fallen crumbs.

Christine approached with my check. "How was your food?"

"Delicious. Thank you."

"Anything else? I'm taking off."

"Busy evening?"

"Finishing a thesis on Contemporary Literature. It's due tomorrow."

"The clash of cultures." I reached for my wallet. "Good luck."

She smiled, nodded acknowledgment. "Anything else?"

"No. Thank you."

Christine pivoted with grace and precision. I gazed up into the evergreen canopy and considered if Christine was alone or if she thinks like me at all. I will never know. I do not ask. But I wondered about the sound of her laughter and the stories she would share, if she had purged her longing in lyrical poems and planned to make her life a fearless master-piece.

# Vulnerable

Chuck loved the way Darla said, "Balloon." The pursed-lip pronunciation transformed her face into a righteous child consumed with dreams of stardom. She would close her eyes, smile like summer and be rollerblading down the Walk of Fame wearing a bikini and blowing bubbles to the breeze. But this wasn't summer and they were not in Hollywood. It was the dead of a New York winter.

Darla pulled the pile of blankets over her head. "I am FREE-ZING," she cried. "Screw the landlord and the damned furnace. This is cruel."

Chuck burrowed beneath the blankets. Darla, bundled in long handle underwear and a flannel nightgown, recoiled into a shivering ball.

"Chuckie." Her teeth chattered. "Your feet are like ice."

"I'll warm you up."

"Forget about it."

He pressed his body to hers. "Come on. Let's stay warm together."

"No." Darla recoiled into the fetal position. "As long as this place is below freezing you are on your own."

"Say 'balloon' for me. Just once."

"Balloon my ass. I can't feel my lips."

"Come on, let me warm you up."

"No." Darla's eyes flared. "First, we'd have to undress, at least partially, and that is not going to happen. Then we'd get hot and sweaty and probably catch pneumonia, but most likely it would be you then I'd have to take care of you. But I don't want to, because it is too damn cold."

"It's Sunday morning."

She disappeared under the covers. "Read the paper."

"What about the call to adventure?" He used a pillow as a prop. "Let's pretend we're in the Himalaya on an expedition to discover the meaning of life. A snowstorm overwhelms us. The wind shrieks and howls. We huddle in our Sherpa tent and have to do whatever is necessary to survive."

"You have lost your mind."

"Come on, let's improvise."

"No. Until we have heat, I am not doing a damned thing."


Their Hollywood romance began in the Acme Comedy Theater. Chuck considered his newfound improvisational skills had wooed Darla beyond reason. He assumed, because she laughed easily, that she had a crush on him. That assumption was challenged the afternoon he discovered her lounging in a BMW convertible, top down, parked in front of California Pizza Kitchen. The driver approached carrying takeout bags wearing skinny black jeans and a Guitar Center T-shirt. A barbed wire tattoo encircled his left bicep.

Chuck muttered to himself. "I could take him."

The driver revved his engine.

Chuck yelled as loud as he could, "Hey, Darla. What's this?"

Darla gestured like a beauty pageant contestant.

"Oh, hi Chuckie."

Traffic edged north on La Cienega. Chuck followed up the sidewalk.

"What is this?"

"Hey Chuckie," Darla shouted. "I'll call you later."

Darla waved. The BMW headed north toward the Hollywood Hills. Chuck zipped his leather jacket and jumped on his Harley-Davidson, but decided not to chase after them. He went home to his efficiency apartment off Hollywood Boulevard, opened a can of Schlitz and waited.

It was almost dark. He sat on the Murphy bed and opened another can, his hunger taunted by a bouquet of aromas drifting up from the street: jasmine rice, carne asada, and pepperoni pizza. Chuck went to the window, took a long drink and watched the palm trees against the fading light. The phone rang.

"Hi Chuckie!"

"That all you have to say?"

"Chuckie is what I call you. Unless you've done something wrong."

"I haven't done a thing."

"You've been drinking."

"Please, don't change the subject."

"I had a glorious day that your sour mood cannot ruin."

"All right." He took a drink. The beer was warm. "What happened?"

"Are you sitting down?"

"No, I am not."

"Sit down. This is big."

He sat on the bed, examined the scar on the back of his hand.

"You won't believe it," she said. "You just won't."

"Darla, please. Say what you have to say."

"Okay. Paul took me to meet his producer in Studio City. I auditioned for a part on the daytime drama *All My Troubles*." She paused then screamed into the phone. "I got the part! Chuckie, I got the part. I'm going to be a star. I just know it. This is my big break. Are you happy for me?"

"Sure, that's great." He squeezed the Schlitz can until it collapsed.

"You don't sound happy."

"What's the part?"

"I play an Italian ingénue plotting to murder Paul's character."

"Do you succeed?"

"With what?"

"Killing Paul?"

"No, Paul has thirteen weeks on his contract. He can't die yet. I'm on for three episodes then disappear with his money."

"I don't see you playing an Italian."

"Honey, I'm an actress. And I have a new voice coach."

"Congratulations."

"Thank you very much. You'd better be ready 'cause I'm coming over to give you an attitude adjustment."

Chuck smelled his T-shirt. "I'm grungy."

"Take a shower, but don't shave." Darla's voice thickened. "Schiavo!"

"Schiavo?"

"It's Italian. It means, 'I am your slave.'"

Chuck liked the sound of that. His mind cleared under the hot shower. He hoped Darla's good fortune was contagious. For six months he was right. Darla got a role in a television movie followed by a cameo in a Weird Al Yankovich music video. Chuck landed a Miller Lite beer commercial that went national. Then Darla flew to New York to audition as an M-TV host. She accepted on the spot.

The afternoon Darla returned from New York Chuck took her for a ride along Mulholland Drive on the Harley-Davidson, her arms wrapped tight around his waist. They stopped to look out over Westwood, Santa Monica and the expanse of the Pacific Ocean. Darla raked fingers through her tangled hair.

There was a long silence. "I'll miss you," Chuck said.

"Miss me?"

"You'll be in New York. I'll be here."

Darla smiled, her teeth perfectly straight and white. "You are coming with me."

He touched her face. "I don't want to slow you down."

"That's silly. We'll move in together." She clutched his hand. "You're my good luck charm. There's tons of work. It will be fun. You'll see."

Chuck pulled her close. Darla kissed him. He sold his motorcycle the next day. They moved across the country into a small walk-up apartment on the Lower East Side. It was the best place they could find. Then came winter.

Darla dozed peacefully under the blankets. Her teeth had stopped chattering. Chuck insulated with layers of clothing, zipped his leather jacket and stepped into the hallway. His breath formed clouds when he exhaled. An elderly couple argued behind the door of the next apartment. Their voices quieted for a moment followed by a loud bang against a radiator. The stairs groaned as he made his descent. Windows in the stairwell landings glittered with frost.

The first floor hallway was filled with the smell of scrambled eggs, bacon and fresh brewed coffee. He inhaled deeply then knocked on the door.

Mr. Burnside, the superintendent who resembled the Wizard of Oz, appeared behind the security chain.

"What's the problem?"

"Heat. We need heat."

Mr. Burnside turned back into the apartment. "Dear, it seems our young Hollywood tenants don't appreciate the change of seasons."

"It's colder than hell in our apartment."

"Really?" Mr. Burnside turned his head. "Dear, our tenant says it's colder than hell upstairs. What do you think?"

Heavy footsteps approached. The door closed. The security chain rattled and the door swung open. Mrs. Burnside pushed her husband aside, her ruddy face clashed with a neon orange hunting cap pulled tight around her ears.

"Got a problem?"

"It's cold. We need heat."

"It's ten degrees outside." She poked a finger in Chuck's direction. "We have a building full of people huddled together, wrapped in blankets and sitting on heating pads. What makes you special?"

"I'm not special. We're freezing, that's all."

"You young people haven't been together long enough to

be cold."

Mrs. Burnside slammed the door. The stairs creaked and groaned with Chuck's ascent. In the apartment, sunlight poured through the frosted windows. He removed his jacket and boots, layers of clothing.

Darla was fast asleep. She rolled onto her side and murmured. A smile broadened her lips and she curled up into a question mark. Chuck slipped beneath the covers, her bundled body warm and welcoming. He thought about Hollywood and orange blossoms, about laughing children and red balloons. Chuck closed his eyes and joined in her dreams.

# Devil's Food

Relaxed on his veranda with a glass of old vine Zin-
fandel, Ozzie enjoyed the sun dancing off his infinity
pool and the unobstructed view of the Santa Monica Mountains. He savored the wine, reflected on his parents
and the early life experience that forged his identity and the
man he would become. In retrospect he confessed Catholic
school was probably not the best place for a willful young
boy named Schwartz. After the sisters whacked his knuckles
a few times he quickly came to understand the consequences
of aberrant behavior.

With a Jewish father and a self-proclaimed recovering
Catholic mother, the church considered Ozzie a limbo baby,
an innocent soul condemned to oblivion. His parents were
not religious people, however, they did believe in education
and Saint Agnes of Rome was the finest school in the San
Fernando Valley. Uncle Tommy O'Brian's construction company had practically donated a new roof for the gymnasium,
an act that assured Ozzie's eligibility.

His intellectual inquisition began in 1965 on the Griffith Park pony ride. His sixth birthday, and too young to be
self-conscious about wardrobe, Ozzie mounted the pony
wearing an authentic Buckaroo Bob costume complete

with cowboy hat, studded vest and furry chaps. A television writer and producer, Mr. Schwartz insisted Ozzie wear proper wardrobe for his first adventure on horseback. The Super 8mm home movie camera whirred as Ozzie bobbed along for a several glorious moments. Following his father's cryptic stage directions, Ozzie tipped his hat, beamed and bobbed until the pony bucked. In an instant Ozzie launched airborne, a furry-legged cartwheel tumbled through space landing face-first in well-trodden pony dirt.

The loss of a baby tooth compounded his humiliation. That night Ozzie placed the separated incisor beneath his pillow in anticipation of just reward for his pain and suffering. Early the next morning Ozzie found a quarter where the tooth had been. He clutched the coin in fist and marched into his parent's bedroom.

"Hey, wake up," he said. "The lousy tooth fairy gypped me."

His parent's didn't budge. Ozzie crawled on the foot of their bed.

"Hey, wake up," he demanded. "I'm here to report a crime."

"What is it honey?" his mother asked.

"I put the tooth under my pillow like you said." Ozzie extended his hand and revealed the coin. "All that fairy left me was a quarter. That's not right. Billy next door got a dollar. He didn't even bleed."

"Honey, maybe the tooth fairy was short on change."

Mr. Schwartz started to come around. "What's this?"

"Ozzie thinks the tooth fairy has been unfair."

Ozzie presented the quarter.

"You should be grateful," Mr. Schwartz said. "Or, maybe you don't need a tooth fairy like other children. Think about that."

Being the son of a writer was a different way of life. Ozzie could never be certain of his father's motivational offerings as every situation could inspire dialogue for a scene in development. That morning Ozzie accepted his father's words as fact and decided he didn't need the tooth fairy. He decided if he wanted something, he'd get it himself. He was soon enrolled at Saint Agnes where his formal education began.

Father Dunegan ruled the school. A large man, balding with Ben Franklin glasses perched on the end of his nose, Father Dunegan patrolled the hallways, hands on hips with a twelve-inch hardwood ruler hidden in his coat sleeve. He often whistled off-key like the soundtrack from a climactic scene in a spaghetti western. The students knew, when the whistling stopped, some poor kid would likely be nailed. Foolishness was forbidden. Punishment came swift and certain.

Ozzie followed the rules and after a few years learned to hold his own. A benchmark he noted on the day his wayward dodge ball smacked ill-tempered Sister Margaret in the head.

"Ozzie Schwartz." Sister Margaret seethed as she grabbed his collar. "I swear you are a child of the devil."

"Forgive me, sister," he said. "It was an accident. And swearing won't change anything."

Sister Margaret released him like an angler who had bagged her limit. On the relative safety of the playground Ozzie took his chances. Inside the classroom another story unfolded. The elderly Sister Consuela, who taught religion, rarely touched the children unless they nodded off in class. "Wake up my dear," Sister Consuela would say. "You can't learn consumed with idle dreams." At the other extreme Sister Margaret, who taught history and girl's physical education, made Father Dunegan seem like Mother Teresa.

The students attended religion class each day. In a lesson she repeated often Sister Consuela explained that angels guard every child. "Above our right shoulder hovers a good angel," she said. "And above the left, an evil angel. We choose between good and evil every moment of our lives."

Ozzie considered dealing with both of those angels a challenge. He wondered how a blessed angel became evil, but never asked. His father cautioned him to study and withhold his contrary opinions.

George Molina and Ozzie became best friends in fourth grade. Tall and awkward, George tended to stutter when he became anxious. Some children teased George and Ozzie understood what it was like to be different.

After school at Ozzie's house the boys played chess or watched Superman or The Three Stooges on television. They discussed the Apollo astronauts and explored back issues of National Geographic and the Sears Roebuck catalog. Their biggest sin involved sharing a sip of Cutty Sark scotch whiskey and choking on a Silva Thins cigarette acquired from Mrs. Schwartz's purse.

On a sleepover George brought a surprise. As soon as Mrs. Schwartz turned out the lights George started sputtering. "Ozzie, wa-wa-wait tttil ya see this." He dug deep into his sleeping bag. "Your na-na-not gonna be-be-believe it." Ozzie flipped on his Cub Scout flashlight. With reverence George presented an autographed black and white photograph of Marilyn Monroe. Ozzie would never forget how Marilyn arched her back and pursed her lips, how her eyes seemed to know what he was thinking.

Ozzie's mouth went dry. The sensations rushing through him were consistent with what Sister Consuela described as the deadly sin of lust.

"She's be-be-beautiful, huh Ozzie?"

"People say she is beautiful and sexy. But look at her eyes. She looks sad." Ozzie lowered the flashlight. "I've seen her in movies. She's dead. She killed herself."

In May there was an assembly. Children brought flowers then filled the stadium grandstand to hear the sixth grade choir sing a selection of popular songs. George and Ozzie had forgotten their flowers. As soon as the performance began they sneaked beneath the bleachers to see what they could find. When the choir finished *Up-Up and Away* the student body stood to applaud. A white rose fell to the ground.

"Ozzie, lo-lo-look." George pointed.

Over their heads, gaps in the bleachers revealed a row of skirted sixth grade girls.

Ozzie turned his head. "We shouldn't be looking," he muttered.

That's when Sister Margaret collared them and knocked their heads together like a pair of cartoon coconuts.

"What's gotten into you boys?" She twisted their collars into knots.

"Na-na-nothing Si-si-sister Ma-Margaret." George stuttered. "Na-na-nothing. I pro-pro-promise."

"Yeah," Ozzie said. "We're looking for flowers."

Sister Margaret glanced up into the bleachers and tightened her grip.

"You're guilty. That's all there is to it."

Father Dunegan sentenced them to three swats and three hours of community service. Sister Margaret watched approvingly as Father Dunegan rose from his green leather chair with hardwood ruler in hand. The boys rolled up their sleeves. George stood with head bowed and prayed. Ozzie tried not to cry as the ruler slapped against his bare forearms.

"I'm so-sorry Fa-father," George said through his tears.

When it was done Father Dunegan reclined in his chair.

"You boys must think pure thoughts. Life's that simple. I do not enjoy causing you pain. Discipline is my duty to God. I suggest you pray. Ask God to keep your minds free from evil thoughts. Remember, '...whatever ye shall ask in prayer, believing, ye shall receive.'"

During recess a few days later George and Ozzie picked trash along the schoolyard fence. George found a small lizard. He tied a string around the lizard's chest, stuck it on his shirt and within a few minutes the reptile was almost white. The lizard seemed content and so did George. When the bell rang George, the lizard and Ozzie hurried to Sister Margaret's history class and took their seats near the back of the room. Sister Margaret pointed to a map of Europe and began a lesson on the Iberian Peninsula. Five minutes into class George turned to Ozzie, pointed at the linoleum floor and the lizard. George attempted to coax the chameleon into his hand, but the lizard scurried along the baseboard toward the front of the room.

"Ozzie Schwartz, is there a problem?"

"No Sister," Ozzie said. "Everything's fine."

"And do you have a problem Mr. Molina?"

"Na-na-no Si-sister."

Sister Margaret slapped the map pointer across the width of Spain.

"Mr. Molina. Why don't you come share what you've learned so far today?"

George froze in his seat. He checked the floor, but the lizard was gone.

"Mr. Molina, we're waiting."

George limped to the front of the room. The students squirmed in their seats. Sister Margaret handed George the pointer and stepped aside.

"Now," she commanded. "Tell us what you know about the Iberian Peninsula."

George's face turned pale. He pointed at the map. "The Ib-ib-iberian Pee-pee-pensula..."

Their classmates laughed.

"SILENCE." Sister Margaret sounded out the syllables. "PEN-IN-SU-LA. Pronounce it correctly."

"PEE-PEE-PENSULA."

"PEN-IN-SU-LA," Sister Margaret insisted.

"Pee-pee-pensula," George said, his eyes filled with tears.

"You will stand there until you pronounce the word correctly." Sister Margaret grabbed George's shoulder. "PEN-IN-SU-LA."

Ozzie watched the lizard dash across the floor, leap onto Sister Margaret's boot and disappear beneath the folds of her skirt. Her eyes grew as big as saucers. She hesitated then went berserk. "DIOS MIOS," she screamed. "DIOS MIOS." She shoved George aside, danced and kicked, shimmied and shook her skirt like a dance hall showgirl.

The students shrieked with laughter. Ozzie began to clap his hands and most of the students clapped along. Sister Margaret jumped and yelped and kicked, screamed and sashayed around the room. Finally George's lizard dropped to the floor frozen with fright. The room fell silent. A few long seconds passed then Sister Margaret's boot crushed the creature.

The students gasped. Sister Margaret's chest heaved. Beads of sweat trickled down her brow. She straightened her skirt, regained composure then marched George and Ozzie to Father Dunegan's office. Sister Margaret stated her case. Father Dunegan excused her, rose from his chair and removed his coat.

George bowed his head, "Pppleeease na-na-no."

Ozzie stepped between George and Father Dunegan. "This isn't right. Please Father, we're innocent."

Father Dunegan stared over the tops of his glasses. "Then explain to me Mr. Schwartz, how that creature came to be in Sister Margaret's classroom?"

"We found the lizard when we were picking trash. It got loose." He lifted his right hand to pledge an oath. "But after that, we're innocent. I promise. How could we train a lizard to climb up Sister Margaret's skirt? That's impossible."

Father Dunegan removed his glasses and rubbed his face. For a moment Ozzie thought Father Dunegan would smile, but he just shook his head. A rare pardon spared the boys the wrath of his ruler. For some reason, that day they got lucky.

When Ozzie's mother picked him up after school that day the car radio played Peggy Lee's *Is That All There Is*. A depressing song so Ozzie turned off the music and told his mother the story of how the ill-fated lizard made Sister Margaret dance. Mrs. Schwartz laughed out loud. Ozzie laughed too, but he never told his parents about the humiliation of George Molina. Ozzie knew his friend believed in God and angels and hoped somehow George's prayers that day had been answered.

The shadows grew long on the veranda. Ozzie poured a glass of wine, marveled at the sunset. He valued the friendship of George Molina and the childhood experiences they shared, the awful first taste of scotch and how Marilyn Monroe's beautiful face appeared so forlorn. Those memories he folded like pages in an aging scrapbook. Absent the subjugation of guilt or shame, through the years his good fortune and healthy desires developed naturally. Ozzie took pride knowing that he survived his passage through Saint Agnes of Rome without the benefit of a single miracle.

# The Reunion of Last Resort

The headline of the *Weekly Resort Times* was set in the boldest type possible: MAYOR'S WIFE AND ELVIS IMPERSONATOR CAUGHT WITH PANTS DOWN AS CLASS OF '68 LOOKS ON. But that's not exactly what happened.

Sometimes I feel like the Rodney Dangerfield of Elvis impersonators. No matter how hard I work, no matter how many miles I log in the interest of Elvis, I can't get the respect I deserve. So why would my twenty-fifth year high school reunion be any different?

If there's anything I have learned from my travels it's that there are two kinds of people in this world, it was true in 1968 and it's true today. There are the people who get respect and those who don't. There are those who have and those who have not. And a mere proximity to the wrong side of the railroad tracks can scar a soul for life. The only reason I was even halfway accepted in high school was my singing ability. At every dance from 1966 through 1968, my band, Johnny Bellew and the True Blues, kept everybody hopping. And, although there might have been some laughter behind my back, the dancing fools even enjoyed the Elvis impersonation I always used to start our second set. How would I know Elvis would die in 1977 and launch my career? I guess I was ahead of my time, an impersonating prodigy longing for some respect.

Over 200 graduates in 1968 marked the largest Last Resort High class. The baby boom resulted in about half our class sitting in prefabricated buildings from elementary through high school. The local politicians would never dare suggest raising taxes to expand schools because of a little post-war population explosion. Last Resort remained, after all, a tourist destination. Everything designed to bring families into the lodges and onto the lake, amuse them, take their money and send them home with reservations for the next season. Preserving the quiet status quo became the foundation of the local economy.

Many of my classmates had graduated and escaped the gravity of the tourist trade. Because of our unfortunate destiny of being born to poor parents, we didn't really have a lot of choice but to leave. Those who remained either inherited their parent's businesses, tried to marry someone that did or went into politics.

The president of our senior class and prom king, Douglas Carson served as mayor of Last Resort and had his mind set on running for his father's old state senate seat. His wife Carol Anne had reigned as our prom queen, and every boy's drive-in fantasy both then and now. The smiling faces of the Carson family had ruled over Last Resort for twenty-five years. And they were the proud owners and operators of the Ozark Heaven Inn, the setting for our class reunion dance.

Enid Ferret photographed the graduates as we came in the door. One of the have-nots who had left town, Enid returned six years ago with enough money to buy the *Weekly Resort Times* newspaper. Editor, publisher and photographer, she eagerly promoted the interests of the local community with the exception of anything concerning Douglas Carson. In high school Douglas and Enid dated, but he dumped her to go back with Carol Anne two nights before our senior prom. I took Enid to the prom, which meant she sat and listened to the True Blues and me while everyone else danced the mashed potato and the boogaloo. The entire evening she sat with legs crossed, grinding her teeth and staring daggers at Douglas Carson and Carol Anne. Enid began to look kind of scary so I asked the boys to play a couple of slow instrumental tunes and we danced.

"I'm going to get even with Douglas Carson if it takes me the rest of my life," Enid said. At the time this surprised me because I'm not a bad dancer. Of course later I figured out she must have really loved the guy, but I can't imagine why.

I arrived late for the reunion. Enid almost dropped her camera. She gave me a big hug, took my photograph and promised we would catch up later. I straightened my sport coat and entered the ballroom filled with the ghosts of days gone by and a disc jockey playing solid gold Sixties tunes by The Beatles, The Beach Boys, and The Rolling Stones. There was a buffet line and lots of balloons and hellos and how-have-you-been. I'm not putting it down or anything, after all these are my roots, my people, the aging sock hoppers who helped make me who I am today. But somehow I expected something more.

I made the rounds and started having a good time catching up with everyone. I tried not to be too conspicuous, which is difficult wearing a white sequined sport coat and my signature Elvis sunglasses. I can't deny I'm an attraction. This is not just my profession. This is who I am.

I warmed up to being there and everything was going fine until Carol Anne Carson emerged from the crowd wearing a pink chiffon party dress clutching a tumbler filled with ice and Southern Comfort. Accustomed to getting whatever she wants in a matter of seconds Carol Anne had me backed up against the wall.

"Johnny, honey you look so good." She slurred her words, wrapped her free arm around my neck and kissed me square on the lips.

"Thank you Carol Anne," I said, pushing her away to keep things as polite as possible. "You're lookin' pretty fine yourself."

And she did look good, unsteady maybe, but good. She put her arm through mine and burped. "Come on," she said. "Let's dance."

"No thanks. I only dance to slow ones, and never with married women."

"Oh come on, loosen up and have some fun." She nudged me into a corner behind some curtains beside a couple of tanks of helium and started playing with my sideburns. "Johnny honey, this may be your last chance. Ever."

"You know me," I said. "When it comes to the ladies I've never been much of a gambler." I tried to maneuver around her, but she was having her say.

"Oh come on, you're a man of the world, aren't you Johnny?"

"I don't understand."

"You've been around, you've seen things. Douglas and I have traveled, but I don't think I've gone very far with him." She looked back toward the dance floor, then up at her face reflected in my sunglasses. "You know what I mean?"

"I wouldn't hazard a guess."

She drank from the tumbler. "A month ago I drove to Kansas City with my girlfriends and we went into this adult entertainment store. I could not believe my eyes. How can a girl live past, I can hardly speak the words, her fortieth birthday and not know there's a whole other world to be explored?"

"I can't answer that."

I should have excused myself, but she pressed against me. I didn't want to be rude or have her fall flat on her face. I stood there and listened.

"I guess I could order from one of those catalogs, but Douglas would have a coronary if the postman delivered a parcel filled with marital aids. He would just die."

"Everybody has always thought of you and Douglas as the perfect couple." I lowered my voice for effect. "Maybe you haven't given him a chance."

"A chance? What would you call twenty-five years?" She tilted the tumbler and took a long drink. "My lips are like rubber, feel them."

"I think it's time to go find your husband."

"To hell with Douglas. He's over there trying to talk Bill Baxter's wife Betty into being his campaign treasurer." She pointed to the dance floor where Douglas and Betty performed the twist like a couple of thirteen-year-olds. "In case you didn't know, Bill Baxter is the county sheriff and Betty's family owns half the valley."

Douglas and Betty stopped twisting, approached the deejay booth and made a request. With a "ye-haw" the deejay proclaimed it time for country line dancing. The dance floor crowd whooped and hollered as if the rodeo had just rolled into town.

"Oh my god, no." Carol Anne turned pale and fell against me. "Country line dancing makes me sick. I think I'm going to vomit."

"Let's get some fresh air."

Without thinking I grabbed Carol Anne and walked her onto the balcony. The country line dancing began with a fevered pitch behind us. A cool breeze came off the lake and the crescent moon appeared from behind high clouds. I held Carol Anne as she heaved and puked over the rail onto the manicured lawn of her Ozark Heaven Inn. When she finished I gave her my scarf. She wiped her mouth. Some color returned to her face, but she still staggered.

"Johnny, what are ben-gay balls?"

"What kind of a question is that?"

"Honey, I want to know."

"You mean 'ben-wa' balls. You roll them in a closed fist for relaxation."

"You're such a liar."

"No, I am not."

"You're lying, but I'll let you make it up to me."

She stumbled against me and tried to slip her hands in the front pockets of my trousers.

"People can see us!" I grabbed her arms.

"I can't believe you. For a guy who makes a living grinding his pelvis, you are so up tight."

"We should go inside."

"But I have a little favor to ask."

"No."

"I'll get down on my knees."

Carol Anne stepped back toward the rail and knelt in front of me. "Johnny honey, I'm begging. Just sing me one song like you're Elvis."

"Please, Carol Anne. Get up."

"I'm not moving until you start singing." She fumbled for my pant legs.

"Okay, but stay there and don't touch. I can't sing if you're touching me."

She lowered her hands. I took a deep breath, twitched my upper lip and began to sing in my deepest Elvis voice, "Treat me like a fool, …" And that's when all hell broke loose.

From behind me flashed a light and then another. I turned to see what had happened. Carol Anne jumped up and lost her balance. The light flashed. Carol Anne screamed and, as I turned toward her, fell backward. Everything went into slow motion. I grabbed her arm. We crashed through the wood railing, clutched each other and rolled down the grassy hill. The lights continued to flash from above. We stopped rolling just short of the lake.

"Are you hurt?" I asked.

"Not sure." Carol Anne groaned. "I think I'm okay."

I helped her to her feet. We straightened our clothes and picked grass out of our hair. Lucky neither of us broke anything. As we struggled up the hill the lights flashed again.

On the landing Enid Ferret stood triumphant clutching her Nikon camera and strobe. Behind her stood most of the class of 1968.

Douglas Carson declared Carol Anne in no condition to make a statement and took her home. Sheriff Baxter considered it his solemn duty to place me under arrest and did just that. "The safety of other decent women in the county had to be protected," he said. Enid Ferret took notes, imagined possible headlines and tried not to laugh.

I spent what remained of that glorious night in the Last Resort county jail. The accommodations weren't bad except for the old deputy snickering and asking me to sing *Jailhouse Rock*, which I refused to do.

Enid had her sweet revenge. She published a special edition. The photographs were spectacular, especially the ones with the camera angle from behind with Carol Anne on her knees in front of me. Enid published the entire spread: Carol Anne and me rolling on the grass with her pink chiffon dress over her head, the two of us wandering up the hill in a daze, the sheriff taking me away. Enid's good fortune became my nightmare.

First thing next morning, Carol Anne called the sheriff and demanded my release. No charges were filed. I proceeded straight to the motel and packed my bags, drove my rental car to St. Louis and took the next flight out.

The editorial in the *Weekly Resort Times* cleared my name. In the next to last paragraph my dear friend Enid wrote: "In fact, Johnny Bellew was only attempting to save the mayor's intoxicated wife from falling to her death. Bellew is a true hometown hero who was falsely accused, the victim of an embarrassed mayor and an overzealous sheriff."

The entire county reverberated in an apparent state of shock. Enid sent me copies of the photos with a note that read: "Thanks for being my friend and making our class reunion such a huge success. Presently, there are no plans for another reunion, but how could we top this one? – Love, Enid."

At least one person from my side of town got what they wanted in Last Resort. As for yours truly, I was happy to be back in Las Vegas where I am appreciated and no one asks me to sing for free.

# End of the Bar

Mitch Larson walked across the Persian rugs to the back of Harry's Bar, removed his raincoat and took a seat with a clear view of the entrance. Frank Sinatra's *It Was Just One of Those Things* drifted from the overhead speakers. Mitch admired the fine Italian posters of ornate Venetian masks. He drummed his fingers on the bar, a nervous habit acquired during the months of counseling and mediation that preceded his divorce.

"Yes sir. What's your pleasure?"

The bartender's rugged face contrasted with his white tuxedo shirt. Mitch shifted his weight on the barstool and noted the man's nameplate.

"Charter 10. Rocks," Mitch said.

The bartender returned with a glass and a bottle. Ice cracked and popped as the amber liquid assaulted the cubes. Mitch raised his glass.

"Cheers to you, Robert."

Robert straightened to full height. "Cheers to you sir." He tilted the bottle in Mitch's direction then presented a bowl of roasted almonds.

Outside Harry's Bar Century Plaza, usually awash in Los Angeles sunshine, slipped under the somber spell of a gray winter afternoon. An attractive young couple strolled in animated conversation. It began to rain. The couple rushed away and the plaza was empty. Mitch finished the whiskey and drummed his fingers.

"Care for another, sir?"

"No, I probably shouldn't." The liquor lifted his mood. "I'm meeting a woman. Probably shouldn't get too tight."

Robert wiped his hands with a towel. "Business or pleasure?"

Mitch cradled the empty glass. "I'm not sure. Could be both." He glanced at the door then checked his watch. "Where are the phones?"

"Around the corner to your left."

"Watch for a tall redhead," Mitch said. "Her name is Tanya."

"I'll watch for her, sir."

Beside the bank of telephones the door to the bathroom stood ajar as an attendant cleaned the washbasins accompanied by the halting smell of bleach. Mitch held his breath as he dialed.

"Echo communications," a woman said. "May I have the number you wish to call?"

"Number, what number?" Mitch said. "This is a credit card call. I've already dialed the number."

"This is the Echo operator. If you wish to place a call, I must have the number."

"Echo? What Echo? I thought this was a public phone." Mitch felt the veins on his temples throb. He took a breath, checked his watch. "Come on. I don't have all day."

"I'm sorry sir. The telephone owner must have changed

long distance carriers. Would you like to place a call?"

"Okay, sure. How much?"

"Please hold. I'll connect you with the Echo rate operator."

"Don't put me..."

The operator placed him on hold. Minutes passed. The attendant finished cleaning and closed the bathroom door. Smooth jazz flowed through the telephone receiver.

"Hello, this is Kevin. You need help with rates?"

Mitch squared his shoulders. "Kevin," he raised his voice. "I'm standing at a pay phone. I've punched all these numbers and now I'm talking to you?"

"Sorry. I can only help with rates."

"Okay, okay. How much to call Palm Springs?"

"Los Angeles to Palm Springs, for the first three minutes, is $7.50."

"Seven-fifty for three minutes? You must be nuts. I'm not paying seven-fifty. This is wrong. This is..."

The line went dead. Mitch slammed the receiver into its perch. "Echo long distance, my ass." In the men's room he washed his face, careful not to soil his tie, and ran a comb through the thinning hair on the sides of his head. When he returned the barroom stood empty except for Robert.

"Any luck?" Mitch asked.

"No, sir. I'm sorry. There's been no one."

Mitch checked his watch. "I'll have another. Make it a double."

Robert poured whiskey into a fresh glass. Vapors formed as the warm liquid enveloped chunks of ice. Mitch fixed his gaze down the length of the bar. Two men in tailored suits took one of the small tables along the wall and ordered Absolut vodka martinis. The men consumed their first drinks quickly. Half way through their second round they ordered a third. Their voices grew louder.

"Wife wants me to take her to *Beauty and the Beast*," one man said, chewing a cocktail onion. "She knows how I hate musicals."

"At least it's not the *Nutcracker*," the second man said. He grinned, lit a cigarette. "I love to watch the Kings and Lakers. Otherwise, all I do's work. But what do I know?"

"Carlo, all you need to know is that you're a sales animal. And the old man loves animals."

Mitch gazed at his half-empty glass. The ice had melted, transformed into the shape of a reclining woman. He thought about Emily, her sweet softness and high-pitched nasal laugh. Near the end of the marriage Emily rolled away whenever Mitch tried to touch her. She would clutch the edge of their king-sized bed and sleep with the covers pulled tight. Mitch spent those long nights staring at the ceiling certain she would never forgive him. For weeks after she left he couldn't sleep. It wasn't enough that he loved her. An honest man would have found forgiveness. An honest man would have found a way to make it work.

Mitch swirled the glass and watched the ice cube figure dissolve into nothing. He downed the drink and returned to the bank of telephones, squinted to read the instructions and dialed.

"AT&T," the operator said.

"I love AT&T," Mitch answered.

"Excuse me?"

"I'll never switch. I'll never leave. Even when I have my cellphone."

"We appreciate your business."

The call was answered on the second ring.

"Hello."

"Bernie, you bastard. I've waited an hour. Your friend hasn't shown. I've blown my whole afternoon."

"Mitch, babe. I warned you. It's a toss up, but Tanya's a real looker. And she's funny in a weird sort of way. I wouldn't lie to you."

"Don't give me that crap." Mitch rested his forehead against the phone. "I'll never listen to you again."

"Suit yourself. If I hear from Tanya, I'll let you know."

Mitch hung up. Through the speakers Sinatra sang *Three Coins in a Fountain.*

"How'd it go?" Robert asked.

Mitch slid onto the stool and grabbed a fistful of almonds. Robert refreshed his drink. "My cousin Bernie knows this woman," Mitch said. "She's written a romantic comedy. Bernie asked if I'd read her script. Swears she's gorgeous."

"Are you a producer?"

"In Hollywood everyone's a producer, if you have money." Mitch lifted his drink. "I'm an attorney, but I know producers. Good ones. Why? Are you a writer?"

"No, but in my work I hear a lot of good stories." Robert polished the bar with a towel. "I had an adventure of my own recently."

"Really? Okay, so let's hear your story."

Robert checked on the men at the table, adjusted his apron and rested his hands on the bar. "I just returned from sailing down the coast with my brother."

Mitch focused on Robert's sunburned face.

"One night, off the coast of Baja, we hit a dead calm. No wind. No moon. Nothing. We anchored. The swells barely rocked us as we went below and crawled into our sleeping bags. About two hours later something bumps the hull. We rush topside, check the rigging and struggle to see with only the anchor light atop the mast. We looked, but there was nothing. Then…"

The men at the table waved. Robert tended their check. Mitch thought about Emily and their last vacation in Puerto Vallarta. The days were long and sunny, the evenings warm. They drank margaritas and danced. By the end of the week Emily's skin was tan and smelled of cocoa butter.

Robert returned to the story. "The water parted right in front of us. This huge black head blasted breath into the air. A fine spray fell across our faces. The orca bared its teeth like it was laughing then swam beside the boat. The dorsal fin was as tall as me. A minute passed. Again the water opened. The orca stared at us, blinked and rolled back into the sea."

Robert shrugged his shoulders and wiped the bar.

"That's it?" Mitch said. "Your brother didn't lose a leg or anything? The whale just swam away?"

"We assumed the creature was curious, attracted by the anchor light."

Mitch finished his whiskey. "Thanks for the drinks." He dropped a fifty-dollar bill beside the empty glass. "You're a hell of a bartender."

Mitch steadied himself as he crossed the Persian rugs. Through the windows he saw a tall woman in a trench coat hurry across the plaza clutching a manila envelope and a pink umbrella. Mitch opened the door.

The woman surveyed the room then turned back. "You wouldn't be Mitch, would you?"

He lingered under her gaze for a few seconds. "I wish that I was." Mitch shook his head. "But I'm not."

Mitch buttoned his raincoat and stepped outside. The cool damp air slapped his face. It was good to be a little tight on such a gray day, he thought, to be free from the burden of idle conversation and other people's problems. Feeling light on his feet, he glided across the plaza in the gentle rain and surrendered to the certainty of winter's solemn embrace.

# Laughing Stock

The audience, faceless silhouettes except for the first few rows, waited unaware that beneath Tanya's cool facade fear pounded at the hardened bunker that surrounded her heart. Exposed by blinding spotlights, she caught a breath and lingered in the unexpected silence that rippled through the room. Rejection in Hollywood provided a crucible, a cauldron of criticism designed to consume the weak and indifferent. Tanya recalled an ex-boyfriend's defiant refrain, a constant reminder that she had scrawled in red lipstick on her vanity: WHO DO YOU THINK YOU ARE?

She would not be denied. "I know." Tanya shrugged, raised the microphone to her lips. "I didn't think that was funny either."

The audience laughed. In the second row a nerdish young man with unruly sideburns stared at her like a lost puppy.

"I don't do impressions. I'm doing well to impersonate myself. I have to be straight with you guys, my name is not Tanya Summer." She folded a strand of reddish blond hair behind an ear. "This is 1996. Summer is a fresh stage name for a classic rock DJ, a weather girl or spokesperson for feminine hygiene products."

Chuckles, she accepted chuckles. "My real name is, wait

for it, Tanya Nussbaum. That's German for 'nut tree' or in West Hollywood lingo 'crazy white bitch.'"

The laughter crested and washed over her in a wave of reassurance. Only a few minutes remained, not enough time to establish a new premise and get the audience back on a roll. She assessed the young man in the second row. "Hey, what's your name? Where are you from?"

The man awoke wide-eyed from his daydream.

"Right, you with the sideburns, tiny hands and harry knuckles," she said. "How's life in the shire?"

The audience laughed. A red light flashed in the back of the room. She had a minute to wrap.

"Lloyd," he said. "I'm from Pacoima."

"Hey everyone, Lloyd lives in Pacoima. That's shire adjacent. I hear they have awesome trailer parks." Tanya slapped her thigh. "Well, hook me up."

Nervous laughter. Lloyd squirmed. "Why are you mocking me?" he said.

"Hello?" Tanya rapped her knuckles on the microphone. "Earth to Lloyd. I have the audience and an amplifier. When you get home, do a self-exam in your doublewide trailer. Mockery is what makes comedy work."

The room convulsed with laughter. Someone whistled. A man in the back shouted, "You're so hot."

"Thank you." Tanya returned the microphone to the stand, raised her voice. "I'm Tanya Summer, crazy white bitch. Come see my show this Saturday. I mean every one of you."

The rush of applause served as affirmation. Flip Garcia, the emcee, took the stage wearing his signature blue tuxedo jacket, denim jeans and sneakers. "Keep it going for Tanya," he said. "She's available for bachelorette parties, as entertainment and security."

The applause faded as Tanya exited the fire door into the alley, the night air cool and damp. She stared at the muddled sky and the glowing streetlamps that lined the road leading up into the hills. She recounted her set and felt a chill, a tremor of vulnerability that reminded her of when she was a small child helping her maternal grandmother hang laundry, those flat white sheets whipped to life in the morning sun.

Her Grandmother sewed Tanya simple dresses and a hooded woolen shawl. "This lambs wool is magic," the grandmother said. "It will keep you warm and dry, protect you from the world when I am not around." In grammar school Tanya wore the shawl except on the hottest of days. Tall for her age, pale and awkward, in high school she learned to dismiss challengers and would-be oppressors with the underlying truth in every joke. She discovered comedy was more about pain than pratfalls, equal parts word play and self-defense.

Tanya thought about the last two years, sobriety and how, shortly after her thirtieth birthday, she took a screenwriting course with UCLA Extension. There she met Chase Heller, a middle-aged comedian and regular at the Laughing Stock, who encouraged her to write and try stand-up comedy. "Your humor is warped," he offered, his voice deep and measured. "Use the contrast with your appearance to full advantage." Raw and unfiltered, that is how she came to the Laughing Stock. The collective two-year process yielded volumes of material cataloged on index cards and, after several rewrites, the dark comedy *Crazy White Bitches of West Hollywood.*

The fire door opened. Chase Heller brought Tanya a club soda and lime. "Nice work tonight," he said.

"I got lost near the end, had to go into the audience."

"Your riffing is solid."

"I have a lot of new ideas." Tanya stared at an emergent palm tree, the ancient symbol of triumph, growing sideways out of the hill. "Praying some dude heckles me."

"What's the latest with your script?"

"Stalled. Can't get anyone to read it."

"Be patient," he said. "Shifting gears, here's a rhetorical question for comedic consideration: What do you remember most about your first kiss?"

Tanya looked past Chase Heller down the length of the alley, the traffic on Sunset Boulevard morphed into a frantic blur. "The mirror was cold."

The comedians arrived early for the Saturday showcase, gathered around the U-shaped bar or chatted with friends on the sidewalk. Tanya sat in a booth by the wall shuffling index cards. Chase Heller and Kirby Skidman watched Flip Garcia post the lineup.

"I'll open," Flip said. "Second up is Skid-mark."

"Please, don't call me that." Kirby's round face soured. He fumbled for a piece of paper. "Use this: A reject from overeaters anonymous, Kirby Skid-man."

"Sure, man. You got it." Flip folded the note into his jacket, turned to Chase. "Your usual intro?"

"Sure. Or surprise me."

Kirby pointed through the window toward the sidewalk.

"Look," he said. "There's my nephew Lloyd, all shaved and cleaned up, and my niece Cindy. Lloyd was here the other night. I think he has a crush on Tanya."

"She roasted his cashews pretty good," Flip said. "He must have enjoyed it."

"Lloyd's all right. Book smart, but he cock-blocks himself."

"Not a bad looking kid," Chase said. "Tanya's dated worse. I'm not sure about that Spider-Man T-shirt, though. Have them sit near the front and see what happens."

"I'll tell Lloyd Tanya loves hecklers," Kirby said. "That could be hilarious."

They retreated to the green room, a rectangular lounge in the back of the club with a mirrored wall and mismatched vinyl furniture that smelled like disinfectant and burned coffee. Kirby Skidman studied a hand-sized stain on the carpet. Trish the Dish Ramos and Wanda Z joined him.

"Look at this stain," Kirby said. "Imagine it's a Rorschach inkblot. What does it say to you?"

Trish crossed herself and smiled. "A sign of good fortune."

"To me it's a squirrel," Kirby said. "Flattened by a truck."

"Definitely some sort of road kill," Wanda said. "An innocent victim becomes a hillbilly brunch."

Kirby's expression coiled in deliberation. "The squirrel didn't watch where it was going," he said. "The streets are paved with victims. That's why it's called asphalt."

"Brother, you are so insensitive." Wanda smiled knowingly. "That why your college tour got cancelled?"

"Who cares? It's not worth it. I'm obese. My knees hurt. Campus thought police are likely to ban overweight self-deprecating comics. They might sit on someone or have a different opinion. Comedy will soon be considered too aggressive. We are doomed to a humorless future."

Trish moved beside Wanda, slipped an arm around her waist. "My friends, they love to laugh," Trish said. "Whether they have college or not."

Wanda pulled her close. "Don't underestimate these young ones," she said. "Especially the sisters. On the stall in this bathroom a girl wrote: My mother made me a lesbian. Beneath that someone wrote: If I gave her the fabric would she make me one too?"

Kirby snickered. "Fair enough," he said. "That's funny. But how do you know they were girls?"

Wanda raised an eyebrow. "Men don't ask for help or directions," she said. "Black, white or purple, color doesn't matter. Men think they know where they are because in their minds they are the center of the universe."

Tanya stood in the hallway, oblivious to their banter, and visualized her performance scene by scene. She rehearsed daily, owning each word, alternating between complete stillness and articulating every movement. Depending on the audience she was prepared to abandon the entire show, a paradox that once terrified and now excited her. The threat of abandonment no longer frightened her, not since her sobriety. In the darkest moments of a drunken haze, laid out on the cracked tiles of a bathroom floor, Tanya discovered she could not hold on to anything for long, not even the pain.

On the overhead speakers Sheryl Crow sang *If It Makes You Happy*. Tanya squared her shoulder blades and hummed along, considered the current female voices that inspired her:

Gwen Stefani, Tracy Chapman, Jewel, and Natalie Merchant. She peaked through the curtain across the darkened room at the stage, the microphone stand bathed in bright light. Servers hurried among the small tables filling drink orders. An usher with a flashlight directed guests into the remaining seats.

Flip Garcia stepped up to the curtain, buttoned his tuxedo jacket. "Nice crowd tonight," he said. "Are you ready?"

"Of course," Tanya said.

Flip marched down the aisle, onto the stage and snapped his fingers. The music stopped. "Welcome to the Laughing Stock," he said. "We have an amazing show for you tonight with some of the funniest people this side of Pasadena. I'm Flip Garcia, your host. Come on, put your hands together."

The ovation ran its course. "Thank you. I'm Cuban, like a cigar or a classic '57 Chevy," he said. "My parents moved to Los Angeles when I was a baby. They longed for freedom and In-N-Out burgers, animal style. My parents had a traditional marriage. All they did was argue about money. Divorce was never discussed. With five kids they couldn't afford it."

A swell of laughter, Flip caressed the lapel of his jacket. "Like my coat? As a teenager my papa told me: 'Dress for success. Not like your boss, but the president of the company.' No hairnets for me. My mama, she was creative. She fertilized the tomato plants with dog food. If you said 'roll over' the salad tossed itself. When we got outta line mama she said, 'Hold your tongue.' That's tough. Try it. Not now, but when you're home hitting your bong. The human mouth produces a quart of saliva each day. Some people handle it better than others." Flip grinned at a gray-haired gentleman in the first row. "Hey man, you're drooling like a dairy cow. Seriously, have a drink."

Tanya observed the audience reaction and mulled over a scene in the second act of her screenplay. Interior. Night. Alone in her living room the protagonist writes on the inside of her forearm with a henna marker: *I border on insanity. I am up against the wall. Accused of crimes of passion, I refuse to take the fall.* Outside, on the window ledge, a feral black cat with wild yellow eyes watches.

A wave of laughter brought Tanya back into the room.

"What a crowd," Flip said. "Next up, this comedian is living proof that fat people don't get laid, they get rolled—Kirby Skid-mark."

Applause. "Thanks, Flip." Kirby adjusted the microphone stand. "Go blow a Cuban sandwich."

Chuckles. "I'm Kirby Skid-man." He slapped his stomach and nodded to a group of women stage left. "Sorry ladies, I'm taken. But I know what you're thinking—it looks like he's in his third trimester. How does he manage his stretch marks? It's a fact: Happy couples gain weight. The wife and I are overachievers. We're so fat we take separate elevators. We have to do something. Our second vehicle is a fork lift."

Laughter. A server brought a tray of cocktails to a second row table.

"I need exercise." Kirby took a step to the right then a step back. "That's it. I'm done. It's helpful to watch what we consume. A 72-ounce soft drink has over 800 calories and 234 grams of high fructose Franken-sugar. Suck down one of those and you can't tell the difference between the rapture and a diabetic coma."

Laughter. Groans. Kirby grabbed his waist.

"I wrapped my love handles in plastic wrap. I broke a sweat. The wife said I looked like leftovers, soggy leftovers. I know, you think I'm putting down fat people. No, that's gravity." Kirby looked down at the stage, his solemn face on the brink of tears. "I lost my wife recently, in an all-you-can-eat stampede at the Buffet Corral. I found her later, scooping from the chocolate fountain."

Laughter. Applause. Seated in the green room, Tanya drifted back to her story, the unsettled scene in the second act. Interior. Night. In a living room filled with candles the girl with henna markings undulates to the syncopated beat of African drumming, her long arms move like serpents. Cut to a close up, her face ecstatic. "No hero will come to save me," she whispers. "My lips will not turn blue. The bedclothes are all turned down, but I no longer wait for you." Someone pounds on the door. The black cat scurries off into the shadows.

Chase touched Tanya on the shoulder. "The crowd is cooking tonight," he said. "You should warm up."

Tanya stood and stretched. Chase waited a beat at the end of the hall then moved down near the stage.

"That was great." Flip slapped Kirby Skidman on the shoulder. "Next up, a longtime regular at the Laughing Stock. A man who looks like he escaped from a religious cult. Give it up for Chase Heller."

Chase stepped onto the stage. "Thanks, Flip," he said. "How about that Kirby? I've known him awhile. He's an innovator. Kirby rotates his bumper stickers: I heart food stamps. Life is finger licking good. My spirit animal is a corn dog."

Laughter. Chase waited. The gray-haired gentleman raised his glass.

"Chase Heller, my name sounds like a Goth fashion designer, a vampire slayer or an exorcist. All of those descriptions would be appropriate for the women I attract. They tend to wear black and appear a pint short of blood. Here's some dating advice, don't date people at work. Wait until you get off." Chase paused for effect. "I'm into serial monogamy. Right now I only eat granola. You learn a lot from relationships. True love means never having to ask: 'Does this feel good or am I annoying you?'"

Laughter followed by applause. Chase bowed, lowered his voice. "Men die nine years earlier than women. Men commit 70% of the suicides. Recognize a pattern? Toxic love can be a killer. Feel you need some excitement? Miss an alimony payment."

The women stage left nodded.

"In Hollywood everyone is stressed out. Some people are one parking ticket away from their next psychotic episode. There's a sign in the DMV that reads: It's a felony to threaten a state employee. That's where I met Sera Tonin. 'Oh, I love funny guys,' she declared. Turns out, her favorite film was not *Dazed and Confused* or *Groundhog Day*, she loved *Night of the Living Dead.*"

Chase struck a pose, combed fingers through his hair. "Sera had her hair styled at the same place as every frugal sociopath, Pet Go. Her glasses were so thick she could see the future, which did not include me. That's okay. Long term I'm not into zombies, behavioral meds or censorship. I'm cage free. I'm not willing to be a trophy husband, not with some-one I met at the DMV. At my age I'd be more like a consola-tion prize."

Tanya listened from the hallway. Minutes passed. Like the girl in her screenplay, she closed her eyes and swayed with anticipation. She visualized her show, allowed the tension to build. Tanya walked the aisle, an unveiled comedy bride pre-pared to give herself away. Next to the stage she took a deep breath, slowed everything down. The clapping continued as Chase Heller passed.

"Give it up for Chase Heller." Flip employed his full-throat-ed announcer voice. "Next, a West Hollywood woman with a wicked sense of humor, please give a big Laughing Stock welcome to Tanya Summer."

Tanya stepped into the spotlight, waited until the room was quiet. "I've been sober two years now," she said. The au-dience applauded. "Thank you. But please keep drinking. I want to get paid. Most girls say they want the fairy tale be-cause that's the only story they are told. That is complete bullshit—boy fairies, girl fairies, princes and frogs, none of that matters. Fairy dust won't pay for rent, therapy or a reli-able bail bondsman."

Laughter rolled to the back of the room. She waited for the audience, looked to the women stage left. "No fairy tales or glass ceilings for me. It's about time for women to write our own stories. When I was drinking I dated controlling men: producers, cops, a puppeteer. There were always strings attached, or handcuffs. I prefer a gentleman like my Uncle Bob, before his liver imploded."

Tanya paused for the laughter, that's when she noticed

Lloyd, clean shaven and sitting stage right with a girl in the second row.

"And ladies, guys don't want to hear the sordid details about your ex-boyfriends. They don't care how many times you tried to shoot him—or that your parole officer is a black belt in karate. Really, guys don't care. Ask them. West Hollywood dates are high maintenance. You can usually tell by the brand of their purse, especially the guys. Around here it's wise to avoid dance moves that involve slapping your ass. That's too provocative."

Tanya executed a few controlled bumps and grinds.

"I don't want to cause a scene, but I will. I came of age in the 70s with the me generation. Malignant narcissism, that's what I call it. Some people are so self-absorbed their talisman is a sponge. Their theme song: ME-ME-ME-ME, ME-ME-ME-ME, it's all about me. How is it different today? Some kids expect a lifetime achievement award for graduating college, with a social studies degree, and a ton of debt. Or a participation trophy when they discover beard plucking is not just a guy thing."

Laughter reverberated off the walls. Tanya savored the vibration, stroked her chin then gestured with a clenched fist to the women stage left.

"Girl power. You know what I'm saying. Question authority, that's my thing. This began as a child when I realized the Easter Bunny was a fraud. My dear grandmother did her best, but I figured, 'What else are they lying about?'" Tanya moved to center stage, made eye contact with Lloyd. "In rehab someone told me they were born again. I said, in an emphatic tone, 'Awesome, I hope your new parents are sober.'

People say they have found God. Well, I didn't know she was missing. I'm pretty chill these days. I do yoga. It's not a religion. We don't practice righteousness or killing."

Lloyd led the response, clapped with hands above his head as if Tanya had just kicked a field goal to win the Super Bowl. "You're killing it tonight," he yelled.

Tanya rolled her eyes and pointed to the second row. "Hey everybody. This is Lloyd, my stalker fan from the trailer parks of Pacoima." She assumed an aggressive stance. "Hey, Lloyd, what's your girlfriend's favorite album? Let me guess, Aimee Mann's *I'm with Stupid*. Wonder why she refuses to kiss you? It's unprofessional, unless you pay extra."

"She's my sister," Lloyd said. "Cindy."

Tanya froze. Her eyes grew wide. "Aha, that explains everything. Cindy is your sister and your girlfriend? Things get pretty kinky up north in the San Fernando Valley, the porn capital of the entire planet."

"No." Lloyd laughed. "She's just my sister."

"Well, then Cindy needs to help her brother out. It's Saturday night in West Hollywood. You are wearing a Spider-Man T-shirt, in public. Where do you shop for clothes, Toys R Us? Let me guess, you still have a Star Wars poster in your bedroom? And you sleep with your light saber, under your millennium falcon bedspread? If your mother had a tattoo it would read: Ask me about Amway. Am I getting close?"

Laughter. Lloyd and Cindy exchanged glances and smiled. The red wrap light flashed.

"Right, I'll add psychic to my resume." Tanya felt the warmth of the spotlights, focused on the faceless forms in the very back. "Some people have 'I'm a nerd, humiliate me' written all over them. I feel your pain, Lloyd. A lot of me generation women put off having children. They're afraid their inner child will be jealous. The weirdest thing happened the other night. I had a laughing dream. I woke up giggling, thinking: When cells divide do they suffer separation anxiety?"

Chuckles, Tanya soaked them in. "I bet that they do." She rose to her full height, slipped the microphone into the stand. "Each of us is a miracle. Be kind to yourself. Give more than you take. That's the least we can do. I'm Tanya Summer, rule your life."

Applause intensified the surge of her emotions. "Let's hear it for Tanya," Flip said as she floated in triumph through the room.

Out in the alley, the night was clear and unburdened. Cheerful stars flirted above the emergent sideways palm, its new-formed fronds rattled in the breeze. Tanya folded her arms around herself and rocked to the tender rhythm of her heart. A heroic smile graced her lips. She imagined a bright spring morning long ago, under the warmth and shelter of a well-worn woolen cape, her grandmother hummed as they hung laundry on the line. She imagined a room aglow with candlelight and a black cat on the ledge, considered all of the abandoned fairy tales and a stranger knocking at her door. The story of the stranger will have to wait. The memory of this moment transcended everything. Tanya would not let it go.

# Turn Around

V al Marino's friends resembled teenage mutants, outcasts from the Hollywood High School class of 1999, all a bit twisted by hormonal angst, the circumstances of birth, and smoking weed. Spring break senior year should have been a party, a raucous road trip to Palm Springs, but not for his crew. When Val learned about Brody's arrest his first instinct was to disappear, to become invisible. He packed a gym bag and left a note for his mother beside a bottle of vodka: Back in a few days. No worries.

Ominous clouds swelled above the San Gabriel Mountains. Val covered his head with the hood of his sweatshirt, studied the eastern sky and considered how the randomness of nature brought him to this place. Unlike a generation of Los Angeles love children Val accepted that he had been cursed at conception, a fact confirmed the previous fall by his mother's dry martini toast. "Happy eighteenth birthday," she said. "You're here because my damned diaphragm slipped. You lucky boy." Late that night Val found her sitting in the darkest corner of the living room. The stereo played Barry Manilow's *Looks Like We Made It*. A car turned off Fountain Avenue. The headlights pierced the bay window and swept across a wall decorated with a Roman cross and a print portraying the horror of Saint Peter's crucifixion. Val thought she had passed out then the glow of a cigarette drifted to her mouth and down into the glazed ashtray he made for her in first grade, blackened through years of use.

Ladonna pulled to the curb in brother Malik's beat down Datsun wearing her pink and black Neutron Burger uniform. The car smelled like onion burgers, French fries and marijuana. Val's stomach growled in a Pavlovian reflex response as he settled into the front seat. Ladonna produced a blunt-sized joint.

"Hit this man," she said. "Shave the edge."

"No, thanks. I need to be clear."

"Val, how come you never smoke with us?"

"When I'm high," he said. "I can only turn left. I don't get very far."

Ladonna shrugged, returned the joint to her purse.

"Where we headed?"

"The bus station downtown."

Ladonna pulled out of the neighborhood, drove east on Wilshire Boulevard, and checked the rearview mirror. "Yesterday after school Brody and Cheyenne say they need money. Malik and I drop them on Fairfax and wait in the car."

"What happened?"

"Cheyenne, he walked up to a large woman in an orange overcoat. Brody grabbed the purse, but the woman she would not give it up. She took the purse and smashed Brody in the head. Police come from the deli next door. The boys did not run. Malik drove off like we did not see."

"Brody knows what I think about stealing," Val said. "And thoughtless punks that litter."

"We said it was wrong. We told them not to do it."

"Brody is an accomplished liar," Val said. "He could implicate Malik or me and think that was an awesome joke, that we'd all forgive him and laugh about it later. Pretend nothing happened. I'm going to lay low with my aunt in Bakersfield."

Every life was a story, Val thought, written one frame at a time like Rocking Bowl black light bowling nights when he hit his marks and kept score while everyone was high as a kite and rolling gutter balls. His friends love to get toasted and, like when their parents were teenagers, eat pizza and listen to Pink Floyd's *Dark Side of the Moon*. If weed made you more intelligent he would do it every day. Every child should know that getting high is avoidance, that the way to cope with reality is straight through.

Behind them the California sunset produced a brilliant orange glow above the Pacific's unseen horizon. When they reached the bus station Val and Ladonna watched a man in a weathered Army fatigue jacket forage in a dumpster next to a Chinese restaurant. Across the street homeless people wandered or camped on the sidewalk, the damp evening air laced with diesel fumes and despair.

Val handed Ladonna a ten-dollar bill. "Everything will work out," he said. "Tell Malik I have your back."

"I will," she said. "And pray that you are right."

In the terminal a young Latina woman cradled an infant. A ragged man hovered near the entrance. Val checked the bus schedule and took a seat between the young Latina and the door. The baby began to paw at the mother's breast. She covered herself with a yellow receiving blanket and nursed. Val relaxed. He closed his eyes. A reassuring sound track played beside him. Slurp, slurp, slurp, the baby nestled in her arms. Slurp, slurp, slurp, and the baby fell asleep. Val lost track of time. He didn't remember being close to his mother or sleeping in her arms. She rarely showed any emotion beyond sadness and cried the Mother's Day he gave her the glazed ashtray. He would never forget that.

The ragged man limped off. In the men's room Val dropped his hood, combed his hair and washed his face. He was drying his hands when the door burst open. Two girls with backpacks entered wearing jeans and U2 tour jackets, their names written in script over their hearts.

"Anybody home?" said Zoe, the shorter one.

Fonda, her companion, had thick black hair and al-mond-colored eyes magnified like an Egyptian princess by eyeliner drawn to a fine point near her temples. Val trembled when she looked at him.

"Hello fresh boy," Fonda said. "Nice hair."

Zoe assessed Val. "The women's room is trashed." She scouted under the stall doors. "All clear."

"It's cool," Val said. "I was leaving."

Fonda winked. "Wait for us," she said.

He grabbed his bag. "I don't want any trouble."

"Really, wait outside. We'll only be a few minutes."

The Latina mother greeted a soldier in a National Guard uniform. The soldier kissed her and rocked the baby. It was after seven o'clock on Saturday. Val could be safe and on the move. All he had to do was board that bus. Instead, without caring why, he covered his head, leaned against the wall, and guarded the men's room door. The girls exited brushing their hair.

"Thanks for waiting," Fonda said. "Have a name?"

"Val."

"Val?" Zoe said. "As in valiant?"

"Valentino."

"Even better," Fonda said. "What's your final destination?"

"Bakersfield."

"No way." Zoe rummaged through her backpack. "We just came from there."

Fonda moved closer. "Where's home?"

"Hollywood."

"Holy synchronicity." Zoe shoved a cigarette between her lips. "That's where we're going. Fonda's cousin Connie is throwing a party at her tattoo studio."

Fonda smiled, raised her hands and slipped the hood off Val's head. "With me," she said. "You don't have to hide."

"I'm not afraid," Val said.

"I can see that," Fonda said. "In your dreamy blue eyes."

Zoe reached for her friend. "Come on," she said. "Let's go."

Fonda glanced at Zoe then turned to Val. "Want to join us?"

Val did not hesitate. "Sure," he said.

They waited for a cab. A cool wind whistled through the downtown buildings, disturbed the damp uneasy air. Zoe puffed on her cigarette. A bus loaded and moved out of the terminal. The homeless campers huddled, secured their tents and tarpaulins. When the cab arrived they jumped into the back seat.

"The Blue Dragon," Fonda said. "On Sunset near Stanley."

"You have money?" the driver said. "Must see money."

Fonda offered a crisp twenty. "This enough?"

"Yes, no problem."

The driver stuffed the bill in his shirt pocket. Zoe withdrew into her headphones, listened to the Flaming Lips on a Sony Discman. When they reached the freeway a flash of lightning illuminated the sky followed by a loud crack and the rumble of thunder.

Fonda grabbed Val's hand. "I love the rain," she said.

"Then you will be happy tonight."

"I like being happy."

Val folded his hand into hers.

"That's an odd thing to say."

"How so? Why would you live without happiness?"

"Most teenagers are miserable," he said. "That's how I see it. They are in the process of becoming, but do not know what. The challenge is to make the most of whatever misery, or opportunity, comes around. You make adjustments. It's either tune in, tune out or idle somewhere in between. Those are the choices."

"Wow, you sound like my dad."

"Is that good?"

"Good enough. Mom says he's a cynic. That he thinks too much. Mom is normal in the best possible ways, but I worry about my dad. He hates his job. That sucks to only work for the money. He talks about how things were different when he was young." Fonda paused. "What about your family?"

"It's just my mother and me. I take care of myself."

Lightning flared and flickered, exposed the broad looming shoulders of the Santa Monica Mountains. Fonda grabbed Val's sweatshirt, her eyes wide with wonder. A steady rain began to fall. Traffic crept along the slick freeway. They exited south on Highland. Val experienced a surge of dread when they turned west onto Sunset Boulevard.

"Something wrong?" Fonda said.

Zoe stowed the Discman in her backpack. "Maybe your hero's getting too close to home."

"It's nothing I can't handle," he said.

On a Sunset side street, a prostitute held an umbrella and negotiated with a man in a Lincoln Town Car. A few blocks further the cab stopped. They stepped into the rain and through a few smokers huddled under the Blue Dragon's canvas canopy. The crowd of noisy patrons drank wine, balanced appetizer plates, and touted their tattoos, the air heavy with the smell of sandalwood incense, ink and antiseptic. Val and Zoe followed Fonda into the back of the studio where they found Connie—mid-thirties, elegant and clearly in command—dressed in a short black cocktail dress. Her flawless ivory skin served as the canvas for an intricate dragon tattoo that began on Connie's lower back then wrapped over the right shoulder and down across her chest.

"Look, my baby cousin Fonda has arrived," she said. "You sweet thing."

Fonda squeezed Connie and made the introductions.

"You kids put your things up in the apartment," Connie said. "And have something to eat."

Fonda led them upstairs into an expansive loft space.

"My cousin is an artist," Fonda said. "She owns the building. These are some of her paintings."

"Oh my god," Zoe said. "They are so amazing."

Zoe and Fonda stowed their backpacks in one of the bedrooms. Val marveled at the large canvases, the subtle contrasts of muted colors. The loft represented a tranquil alternate reality, a break from the boisterous party below. The long blackout curtains were pulled aside. Rain ran down the plate glass windows that faced west toward the bright lights of the Sunset Strip. Val thought about how he had followed his instincts and how that had brought him to this point.

"Let's have some food," Fonda said.

"I'm not all that hungry," Zoe said. "I'm going to find a cigarette and flirt with the boys."

Val and Fonda made a meal of vegetables and falafel, pita bread and hummus. A reluctant conversation began with Evan, one of Connie's featured stylists, who claimed to have a dozen piercings. Evan fingered his stainless steel nose ring and revealed the bolt pierced through his tongue.

"I love to visit family and friends back in Topeka," Evan said. "You can imagine the looks on their faces. For me it's a scream, but I'm worried they no longer think my tattoos and piercings are shocking. Somehow they have turned out to be sympathetic, like they have Stockholm syndrome."

"What's more to be done?" Val said.

Evan tugged on an earring. "Augmentation," he said. "That's the logical step. I could have my ears modified to look like Mr. Spock. I love Star Trek."

"You must," Val said.

Fonda expressed disbelief. "What are your parents like?" she said.

"Mother is a trial attorney. Father is a psychiatrist."

"It must have been difficult," Fonda said. "Growing up in

Kansas with parents like that."

"We had our moments." Evan waved to someone. "Excuse me. I have to mingle."

The party-chatter volume escalated. The crowd surged. Val turned to face Brody, a bruised gash above his left eyebrow. They stared at each other for a few tense seconds. Val offered his closed fist in a gesture of solidarity. Brody paused then responded with a forceful fist bump.

"Valentino," Brody said. "What's your story? I heard you cut out."

"I went downtown. That's all." Val reached for Fonda's hand. "Ladonna said you guys got busted."

"You can't listen to her." Brody nodded to acknowledge Fonda, raised his voice above the noise. "That scene on Fairfax was totally bogus. I explained to the cops we were helping that old lady. She dropped her purse and overreacted. She assaulted me. Look at my face. Anyway, it was our word against hers."

"What about Cheyenne?"

"The cops took us home. The old man kicks Cheyenne's ass pretty hard. You know the drill. We won't see much of him for awhile." Brody touched his wounded forehead. "This place is like a mosh pit. Listen, I may hook up with Malik and Ladonna later. They scored a fresh bag of Midnight Special. We're going to chill with some tunes and see what happens. Come over."

"Not tonight," Val said. "I'm not in the mood."

Brody shook his head. "Whatever man. You're loosing it." He glanced at Fonda and turned into the crowd.

"Why do you hang out with that guy?" Fonda said.

Val watched until Brody reached the door. "We grew up together," he said. "Our friendship is about all that he has."

Fonda placed her hand on Val's hip and nudged him toward the stairs. In the loft she closed the door, the room dark except for the Sunset Boulevard lights coming through the windows. They sat on the couch and watched the storm.

"I love the rain," she said.

"I know. It makes you happy."

Fonda ran her fingers through Val's hair.

"Yes, but so does sunshine and palm trees," she said. "And the shadows of mountains that grow long late in the day."

Val closed his eyes.

"What's next with your life?"

"I've applied for design school," she said. "Beginning this summer."

"Fonda designs will be bold."

"And you, Valentino, what's your plan?"

"Los Angeles City College in the fall. I'm going to be a teacher."

"You will make a good one."

Val took a chance. He moved his body onto the couch and rested his head in Fonda's lap. Raindrops gathered on the plate glass windows and streaked downward tinted with splinters of colored light. Val thought about the young Latina in the bus terminal and the way she nurtured her child. He looked up at Fonda. She caressed his face. In that instant, with that first tender touch, he realized why his mother drank and how his circle of mutant outcast friends came to be. At some traumatic early childhood moment, or series of acute life altering events, the trust and innocence of each person becomes twisted or torn away. Those are wounds that cannot heal themselves.

# Claim to Fame

C elebrity aspirants rarely appreciate the gravity of their situation until they are offered a promotion at a dead-end day job, forget what happened Burning Man weekend or, once they achieve status, find their ill-fated photo going viral and plastered on page one of the tabloids. Paparazzi feast on cellulite, wardrobe malfunctions and the prized getaway shot from the West Hollywood Sherriff Station. While devouring a Pink's chilidog posed on the bumper of a Toyota Prius may seem like a playful and ironic stunt, such photographs can be a fiasco.

Gravity is the fundamental law of physical attraction. It's unavoidable, like star-crossed method actors and adult children of alcoholics looking for love in hot yoga classes, codependents anonymous meetings or medical marijuana dispensaries. In Hollywood there is always an abundance of cash on the line. The fallen are often the most eager and redemption may present Oscar-worthy opportunities. When a physical intervention is required, I want to get the call. I am Sid Sherwood, body coach.

Avoiding tabloid scandals and rehab aside, my work is more aligned with family counseling than personal training. There is intense pressure to fuel the star-making machine so

I don't begrudge paranoia or odd behavior unless it involves binging on diet pills, pound cake or high fructose corn syrup. If you make a living selling yourself in Hollywood you've earned the right to be eccentric. Privacy is another matter.

On Mondays, after early clients, I enjoy riding my mountain bike through Griffith Park. Weekday mornings the park is less crowded so I may be aggressive without barking "on your left" every fifteen seconds to warn the power walkers and wayward pilgrims. On this hazy morning my internal mind-clearing monologue wrapped when I returned to my Jeep, loaded the bike and took a long drink of water. A pair of foraging mule deer, forced to roam by the protracted drought, paused to watch from the hillside.

I drove back to Jerome's Famous Gym, my training base of operations. Jerome and I were roommates at Cal State Northridge where we studied kinesiology. He played basketball for the Matadors until he shredded his right ACL the semester we graduated. That was ten years ago and when we hatched our plan for a gym specialized in sports performance. Tanning beds were never considered.

Headed west on Sunset Boulevard I saw Jules Marlow strike a pose in front of the Over and Out Burger as her friend Peter took a photo with his smartphone. Jules sported a black yoga outfit with a large Om symbol over her heart and striped knee socks that ended in a pair of fluorescent orange cross-trainers. Her Oz-inspired fashion choices, untamed blond hair and John Lennon-style sunglasses begged the question, "Who is that?" The sunglasses established wardrobe continuity, but I have seen her eyes. They are cool and granite gray until she smiles.

We met in Jerome's parking lot before her 11:00 session. Jules exited Peter's weathered Land Rover holding a Trader Joe's tote bag and a soda.

"Hey Sid."

"Hello Jules," I said with an indifferent nod to her companion. "So you know, a 16-ounce soft drink is the caloric equivalent of twenty minutes on the treadmill. Do the math. That is not on our menu."

Jules lipped the straw and peeked over her sunglasses in a casually innocent flirtation. "Don't jock block my morning bliss," she said. "It's only diet."

"Work the plan, Jules. Drink water."

"Yes, sir," she said, the affirmation laced with lyrical sarcasm.

Beyond the few who have made it big—they must remain anonymous for reasons both ethical and legal—most of my clients either want to be a star or look the part. It certainly helps to have great genes. Jules appears much younger than her age with wide casting potential from feature films to daytime drama. Her agent asked me to prep for pilot season: toned, not defined and a comfortable size two. As a health and fitness professional, and a man, I do not advocate women going for size two or zero, but that's the harsh boney reality of the starlet job description.

Peter leaned out of the Land Rover, pulled a flute-sized e-cigarette from his jean jacket and took a long drag. When he exhaled a hookah lounge volume vapor cloud enveloped the flat brim of his cap then disappeared. The distinct smell of spearmint lingered in the air.

"Hey Sid, Jules an' me we made a bet." Peter had been in

the States long enough for his Cockney accent to mellow. "If I eats an Atomic Double cheeseburger in four bites, she'll buy me lunch."

I noted the breadth of Peter's crooked grin and exercised restraint. "That's not a bet I would take."

"Bloody hell, Sid. Don't spoil me action."

"Action?" Jules flashed a glare of disdain. "In your dreams. I will see you in an hour. Come on Sid, let's get to work."

Late Wednesday afternoons I play pick-up basketball at the Hollywood Y.M.C.A. on Hudson. It's a decent place to network. Sometimes I volunteer with the after school program, but mainly I go to play ball. That's where I met Stanley Mendelson, the motivational speaker and best-selling author of *Your Need to Exceed.* In his early fifties, Stanley is short and stocky with the fearless energy of a Jack Russell Terrier. When you pass him the ball he loves to drive hard into the lane. After a game we spoke.

"Sid, you're in terrific shape," he said. "And a team player. Forgive me for not asking sooner, but what's your line?"

I delivered the elevator pitch. "I'm a body coach, performance and nutrition training with a purpose. I work out of Jerome's Gym off Sunset."

A bead of sweat hung on the end of Stanley's nose. He did not flinch as his flushed red face morphed into a hyper-analytical haze.

"Have you read Norman Vincent Peale?"

"Sure. My father gave me a copy of *The Power of Positive Thinking* when I was in high school. Peale was like the Tony Robbins of his day."

"One could say that. In the landscape of the mind every generation stands on the shoulders of those who came before. We cannot hesitate to take what we need to make our mark." Stanley wiped his face with a towel and stared across the basketball court. "What type of clients?"

"Mostly entertainment. A-list, B-list or walk-ons."

"Older people?"

"Some," I said. "But you are far from old."

"Thank you. And well played." He smiled, paused to consider something. "My wife Lena and I are adding an exercise room. We need some equipment and expert advice. Come up to the house and take a look."

The Mendelson's have a sprawling mid-century modern home on Mulholland Drive overlooking the Los Angeles basin. Beyond the security gate I found a slender woman wearing a white Chanel warm-up suit, linen gloves and a wrap-around sun visor, her silver-blond hair tied back with a pink bow. She clutched a small poodle. Both appeared fresh from the salon.

"Hello Sid, I'm Lena." She offered a gloved hand. "Welcome to our home. Stanley tells me wonderful things about you. And he's an astute judge of character. When you're finished visiting will you have time to take a walk with me and Sophie?"

"Yes, of course." The dog snarled as I shook Lena's gloved hand.

"Forgive Sophie," Lena said. "She was traumatized when the coyotes ate her sister Sasha. That's why we don't walk alone."

"That is horrible."

"Nature can be so cruel. Time is even worse." Lena paused, stroked Sophie. "Stanley is out by the swimming pool. He's easy to find, just follow the noise."

At the back of the house clear plastic sheeting hung in a doorway with floor to ceiling glass windows on either side. Posed like the star of a home makeover TV show, Stanley wore coveralls, a hardhat and safety goggles. He focused on the low wall that divided the room, raised a sledgehammer and crashed it into the structure. Chunks of plaster scattered across a canvas tarp. I knocked on the doorframe.

Stanley looked up and lifted the sledgehammer. "Take note, Sid. When something gets in your way you either negotiate or you knock it down."

The sledgehammer smashed into the wall. Plaster went flying.

"Is this part of your seminar track?"

"Research, my friend. Research." He half smiled then removed the goggles. "I enjoy working with my hands. Besides, the contractor didn't show. I'm not one to wait around. This needs to get done."

We went out by the pool. A breeze swirled up from the canyon carrying the smell of parched eucalyptus. In the distance the marine layer hung like dusty gauze draped over Century City, the Pacific Ocean shining somewhere beyond.

Stanley tossed a hand-sketched floor plan on the table. "Now that Lena refuses to walk the dog alone, we need a treadmill wide enough for both of them."

"You have the space."

After we discussed their preferences I recommended a

dealer for the treadmill, rowing machine, functional trainer, free weights and benches. We scheduled an appointment for fitness assessments.

"Sid, this went just as I expected. Thank you." Stanley offered a fist bump and grabbed his goggles. "Enjoy your walk."

On the dirt fire road Lena held Sophie on a short leash. We maintained a moderate pace interrupted whenever the dog paused along the way.

"Stanley and I have planned to convert one of the guest rooms for some time," she said. "After that tragedy with the coyotes, I insisted."

I did not want to hear the gruesome details. "You and Stanley appear fit."

"We make an effort, but we've been so busy with the business. We're either here writing or out on the road. We've worked hard and been blessed. Now we plan to spend more time at home."

About half a mile out we passed the remains of a house burned in a brush fire.

"The owners barely escaped with their lives," she said. "It happened so quickly. We're grateful the fire station is close."

We picked up the pace. Nothing more was said until we arrived back at the house. Lena asked that I wait on a bench in the shade. She returned carrying a tray with Evian water and a pair of leaded crystal goblets.

"Sid, I have a question." She cupped her hands and squeezed lemon into her water. "I won't be offended if you refuse."

"Ask away."

"Do you know Clay Harmon?"

I did, oddly, from family Trivial Pursuit nights. "The Olympic athlete who became an actor. In the early 60s he starred as the great white hunter in the serial adventure *Dark Jungle.*"

"Yes, that's right. I love it when young people are culturally literate." Lena clutched Sophie's leash. The dog rested beside her. "Clay is my older brother from father's first marriage. We've never been close what with the age difference. When I was a child he did well for a while and was quite popular with the ladies. His career faltered when he began drinking heavily. Maybe the drinking came first, I'm not really sure. A shame because he had every advantage."

"How may I help?"

"Clay lives in a retirement hotel in Santa Monica. Father's trust pays the expenses. I do my best to visit, but over the years he has become somewhat of a recluse. I thought you could meet Clay and encourage him to be more active. I can't stand the thought of him wasting away."

"How is his health?"

"He won't say. Clay's in his eighties, but his mind is sharp to a fault." She stared down the driveway toward the security gate. "Do you think you could give it a try?"

"That would be an honor."

Jules rushed into the gym wearing a slate blue theatrical long sleeve leotard with tights and a flaming pink infinity scarf, her hair twisted and secured with an enameled chopstick. Peter followed several steps behind.

"Sorry I'm late," she said. "I had an audition for *The Young and Relentless* as a dance-obsessed graduate student."

"Nice work," I said. We exchanged a high-five and our fingers entwined for a few long seconds. "How did it go?"

"I think they liked me. We'll see."

"Be confident. You have everything to gain."

Jules smiled. For a moment I thought she blushed, but she turned to her companion.

"Peter's come along. Is that okay?"

"Why not?" I said half-heartedly. "We'll make it a two-for-one special. Suit up."

The twosome spent ten minutes on elliptical machines then I led them through a protracted sequence of modified lunges, squats and twists with medicine balls to promote balance and core strength. We moved to the free-weight area where Jules grabbed a pair of five-pound dumbbells.

"Sid, I have to confess. I haven't been jogging. This week's been crazy with the new apartment, headshots and I had two calls for modeling."

"Focus on your breath and technique," I said. "Maintain a deliberate pace. Make every rep count."

Peter, breathing heavily, returned a set of twenty-pounders to the rack.

"What do you say 'bout the old diet?" he asked.

"I recommend leaning toward Mediterranean. Eat fresh and eat slowly. Avoid highly processed food. Keep it simple."

"Don't me daily duties count for somethin'?"

Jules stepped in. "Maybe," she quipped. "If one were to actually do something."

"Bloody hell, Jules. I play me guitar at least two hours a day."

"If we want definition and results that requires motivation," I injected. "You have to want it. You have to create a sense of urgency."

"That's right, Peter. You have to want it." Jules racked her dumbbells and turned to me. "Sid, do you think I'm motivated?"

I understood this question as analogous to jeans making a woman appear fat.

"Yes, you are definitely motivated. No doubt."

Peter moved behind her. "Stroke a good karma Jules found you, eh Sid?" He rolled his gym towel and snapped it at her hip.

"Hey, watch it." Jules' tone turned south. "I can't afford any DAMNED BRUISES."

She snatched the towel and tossed it in Peter's face. It hadn't registered before, but that spontaneous exchange demonstrated Jules' serrated edge. Her voice and body shifted effortlessly from a moment of self-doubt to one in which she became defiant, and in a charming way, almost dangerous.

"Yes Peter, let's not damage her," I said. "That's not our objective."

"And don't forget." She glared at Peter then turned to me. "And who's side are you taking?"

"The side of progress," I declared. "Always."

Jules and Peter stretched and then moved to their respective locker rooms without further incident. When I checked my cellphone Lena Mendelson had texted that Clay Harmon awaited my arrival.

In the weekend summers of my childhood, when the afternoon temperature climbed near 100 degrees in the San Fernando Valley, our family would often escape Encino through the Sepulveda Pass to Santa Monica where it was at least 20-degrees cooler. I recall homeless people resting in the shade of Palisades Park, how mother would take my sister and me by the hand and dad would say flatly, "Those men have lost their way." I recall the careless seagulls that circled high above our heads. Standing on those cliffs with the wind whipping up off the ocean I could see the arc of the horizon, how the earth was indeed round like the illuminated globe in my bedroom.

A Spanish colonial-style building, the Royal Dolphin faces west at an angle off of Ocean Avenue warmed by afternoon light and guarded by the gentle sway of palms that line the street. An Asian gentleman in a blue linen suit tended the reception desk.

"Hello," I said. "I am here to see Mr. Harmon."

The man stood with a polite and abridged bow. "I am Mr. Lu," he said. "Who are you?"

"Sid Sherwood."

"Yes, yes." He nodded and examined a clipboard. "You are expecting. Walk this way."

Mr. Lu marched with military precision up a wide stairway to a balcony that ran along the face of the building. The residents reclined in a row with their lap blankets either asleep or taking in the view. Mr. Lu pointed to a man with uncombed white hair wearing glacier sunglasses at the end of the row.

"There Mr. Harmon. Good luck."

"Mr. Harmon?" He didn't move. "Hello, Clay Harmon.

I'm Sid. Lena Mendelson sent me."

The recliner creaked under his weight. He stirred, offered the firm grip of his right hand.

"Hello Sid. Welcome to the elephant's graveyard." He fumbled with the pocket of his khaki shirt, retrieved a pack of Camel cigarettes and a Zippo lighter. "Don't mind if I smoke, do you?"

"Yes I mind. Besides, isn't smoking illegal in Santa Monica?"

"To hell with that. This is my only remaining vice." He held the cigarette beneath his nose. "Something seductive about them, don't you think?"

"I wouldn't know. I've never smoked. Tobacco is completely self destructive."

Clay started the cigarette with a flip of the lighter, cocked his head to exhale. "When it's their time, old bull elephants go off to die alone." Smoke drifted from his nostrils. "Researchers say, being empathetic, the aged elephants don't want their friends to witness their demise. During the next migration the elephants come around when the bones are bare and bleached. They fondle their friend's bones with their trunks as part of their mourning."

"How long has it been since your last trip to Africa?"

"What?" He coughed into his fist. "I've never been to Africa. I watch the National Geographic Channel."

"What about *Dark Jungle*."

"Those were filmed on sound stages in Hollywood. Sometimes we'd go on location in Malibu Canyon."

I stood and waited upwind until Clay coughed and crushed his cigarette into the ashtray.

"So, Sid, why are we here?"

"That's up to you. But I suggest we start with the cigarettes."

"I'm too old to quit."

"You're never too old. The benefits are almost immediate. It's a matter of will."

Clay removed the glacier sunglasses. The skin beneath his eyes sagged, but even with decades of sun damage he retained a semblance of rugged good looks.

"You sound like Stanley." He cleared his throat and leaned forward. "There are far worse things than cigarettes. Give me a hand. Let's take a hike."

"Does your doctor say it's okay?"

"To hell with him. What remains of my life is not his concern."

I pulled Clay to his feet. With the aid of a cane we shuffled to the elevator then crossed the street to Ocean Avenue and along the path through Palisades Park. We passed a homeless man with a shopping cart rummaging though a trash bin. Further on a group of women practiced yoga on the lawn.

"I don't see that well anymore." Clay stopped to watch the women moving through sun salutations. "They say I'm legally blind. That's a pisser because they took my driver's license."

I held his arm. As we walked along I recalled the aging of my grandparents, how their eyes grew dull, the crepe of their skin and how, at holiday gatherings, the passing years weighed upon their bodies. They stooped, cupped a hand behind an ear and asked us to speak up, yet they were always joyful in our presence. When Clay and I reached Wilshire Boulevard we turned back, moving slowly along the path.

"How are your eyes, Sid?"

"Twenty-twenty."

"I bet you drink carrot juice."

"Only if it's fresh."

"Fresh, that's swell. You are a regular Captain America. How about women? A clean-cut young guy like you ought to carve a lane with the ladies."

"That's personal."

"Well cha-cha-cha." Clay clicked his teeth like a cartoon character. "You must not be getting any."

"That's not your business."

"And what's your business Sid, walking octogenarians around the block?"

"You don't have to act like a jerk."

"Jerk, huh? Must have hit a nerve. I've been called worse."

"I won't argue with you about that."

We paused when we neared the Royal Dolphin, the building aglow in the waning light with the palm tree shadows animated by the breeze.

"Sorry kid. I wouldn't push the needle unless I thought you were all right. I figured you could take it."

"I can take it."

"Good on you. I hear today these independent-minded young ladies place a premium on sensitive guys, especially one with a job. But you probably don't need advice from me."

"You are correct. I don't."

We crossed the street. I guided Clay through the lobby to the elevator then back to his recliner at the end of the balcony. The ocean breeze freshened, brought a damp chill as the sun disappeared behind a bank of clouds. I draped the blanket over his legs.

"There you go," I said. "That was a good start. I'll come the day after tomorrow and we'll do it again."

"Knock yourself out." Clay reached in his pocket for the cigarettes. "Hell knows I'm not going anywhere."

We walked on alternate days for two weeks. Clay's prickly demeanor moderated as he gained confidence and his strength returned. I've learned not to take it personally when clients begin unloading their emotional baggage. I understand they need to release whatever is holding them back. My job is to encourage them to keep going. Sometimes that is all they want or need. Clay and I moved from the path through Palisades Park to the Royal Dolphin's heated courtyard pool where he exhibited traces of an aggressive freestyle form. After a session we rested on a ledge in the shallow end.

"You are making great progress," I said.

"I bet you say that to all the girls." Clay squinted at the swath of midday sun reflected off the pool. "Yesterday I only smoked three cigarettes."

"Is that good?"

"No shit, Sid." He was indignant. "After a meal, that's when I want it the most. I used to smoke a pack a day, more if I played gin with Murray Gold. Before my eyes went south nobody around here beat me. Now Murray wins and acts like he's some kind of card shark."

Clay coughed and cleared his throat. I wrapped a towel around his shoulders.

"With the smoking it's a wonder you're still alive."

"You don't play gin do you?"

"No. I'm not a card player."

"You don't drink, don't smoke and don't play cards. So, what does Captain America do for fun?"

"Anything that breaks a sweat."

"Right. You're a sports guy." Clay pulled the towel tight around his shoulders. His brow furrowed. "How'd you like to do me a real favor?"

"That's what I've been doing."

"No, no. This is the purpose, as you like to say. It's something I've put off. It may be too late. Hell, I don't know."

"I need more information."

"This may sound strange. I'm only asking because I trust you. Or maybe I just don't care. Somewhere trust and resignation must converge. That's about where I am."

"Go on."

"There's someone I want to see, but from a distance. I want to know the person she's become. I need to borrow your eyes."

"What am I supposed to do?"

"Drive and describe what you see. You'd have to get the address, then we'll sit in the car and wait."

"That would be stalking."

"Hell, Sid. Where's your sense of adventure? Why don't we just call it a stake out?"

"For that you need a private investigator."

"No, that pig won't fly. We'll be okay if we keep a low profile. Ask Stanley to give you the address for Mercedes Cruz. He'll understand."

"Mercedes Cruz?"

"Right. Do I need to spell it?"

"Why don't we ask Lena?"

"No, not that. Lena will raise Cane and tell me all about it. Last I heard Mercedes had a condo on the Westside. Stanley will know."

"I'm scheduled to see him this afternoon. If I'm lucky I'll swing back later."

I walked Clay back to his room. When we reached the door he squared his shoulders and shook my hand.

"I know I'm a hard case," he said. "Thank you."

Stanley had fired the contractor and completed the exercise room with the help of Rodrigo, his Guatemalan gardener. I agreed to a final check of the floor plan measurements before the equipment arrived. Sophie stood in the doorway wagging her tail as I maneuvered on hands and knees sliding the tape measure across the floor. Stanley marked the equipment positions with pieces of masking tape.

"How are things going with Clay?" he asked.

"He gets stronger each week."

"Good. Lena has been worried."

I confirmed the measurements for the last piece and tossed the tape in my backpack. "There's something else. This puts me in an awkward position because Clay does not want Lena to know."

"We're safe. It's Saturday afternoon. Lena is down at the Beverly Center with her girlfriends. What is it?"

"Clay wants the address for a Mercedes Cruz. He said to ask you in person."

Stanley shook his head then left me in the room with Sophie wagging her tail. He returned after several minutes with an address and telephone number.

"The attorney said she still lives there," he said. "But Clay's right. We should keep this to ourselves."

"Is there a restraining order?"

"Nothing that serious. Clay hasn't seen Mercedes in years. If you want the details you'll have to ask him."

I waited at the traffic light to turn onto Laurel Canyon when a text message came from Jules: URGENT. MEET AT GYM. I found her in the lobby wearing a tuxedo and a pair of red Converse All Stars, her hair pulled back tight. She had been crying.

"Jules, what's wrong?"

With a lunge she wrapped my neck in a hug that rivaled a submission chokehold. Her skin smelled of roses and vanilla.

"I feel like I've hit a wall."

"You'll be all right," I said. "If you really want pancakes or a slice of cheesecake, go for it. It's the weekend. You've earned a splurge."

"Please, don't make me laugh."

"You can always be a character actor. They love to eat cheesecake and cherry pie. I see them do it all the time at Canter's Deli."

"Stop. You're not being fair."

"Why should I be fair?"

"Because, I'm trying to be serious."

"Dressed like that?"

She stepped back, took a deep breath and challenged me with the intensity of her gaze. "Something happened," she said. "I wasn't sure if I was hurt or disappointed, but I desperately wanted to talk with someone who would understand. When I thought about where I could go and the people I know I realized that person was you."

As a certified fitness professional my inclination to retreat from personal entanglements became fully engaged, but I resisted.

"Tell me what happened?"

"Peter, you know, took me to a costume pool party in Los Feliz. His wolf pack friends start drinking early on Saturdays. Today their cute little trick was they only asked the girls to wear costumes. Most dressed like vampires or zombie groupies, as one would expect. Around the pool a couple of the guys started playing grab ass. You know musicians?"

"No, I don't." And I didn't. I had heard this excuse veiled in a question on countless occasions and, not being musical, wanted to ask a woman who would know the answer. "Why do musicians always get a free pass for bad behavior?"

Jules smiled knowingly. Her gray eyes sparkled. "Sid, they make the music. But hear me out. I was nursing a Virgin Mary and chewing celery when I had this strange revelation. Before we met, if I was at a party, I would be doing Jell-O shots and craving chocolate fondue. But not now."

A rush of gym members entered the lobby for the studio cycling class. Jules and I retreated to an empty sales office.

"Jell-O shots?" I asked.

"Yes, they can really sneak up on you," she said. "But I'm reformed."

"Congratulations, but what's strange for me is what you are wearing."

"The tuxedo? Two summers ago in Laguna Beach I played a cross-dressing butler in a mystery dinner theater. I kept this thinking it would come in handy." She dabbed her cheeks with a sleeve. "Oh, my mascara has run amuck."

"Why the tears?"

"Peter's drunk friend Gordon, the biggest ass grabber, said I looked like a dyke. I wasn't offended, but he kept saying lesbians turn him on. How original, right? Lipstick lesbians are like every drunken dude's fantasy. Peter just stood there sucking his e-cig. Then this sweet pregnant girl walks through the gate and Gordon shouts, 'Hey, who invited the fat chick?' That's when I lost it. I stepped back and side-thrust kicked him in the solar plexus. Not hard enough to kill him, mind you. When his ass hit the pool the girls all cheered. The guys laughed. The pregnant girl offered me a ride. Gordon's lucky I wasn't wearing heels."

I curbed the urge to laugh and attempted to gather my thoughts, a substantial task given my newfound awareness of her ninja skills. Considerations ran wildly contrary to my commitment to relationship neutrality and well-defined professional boundaries. I followed my instincts.

"What are you doing?" I asked. "Right now."

Jules appeared surprised. "I thought we were having a conversation."

"We are definitely having a conversation and I want to hear every word, but I am on a mission. Do you want to come along?"

"Sure," she said. "Give me a second to fix my face."

In a few short minutes she emerged from the locker room as if nothing had happened. We climbed into the Jeep. I cued her on the Clay Harmon backstory and turned south on Highland toward the Santa Monica Freeway.

"I know this may sound weird," she said. "But I like old people, especially the ones that haven't gone sour."

"Well, Clay is a trip. When we get there, just be yourself."

"I do that every day. Don't worry, I won't embarrass you."

"That is impossible."

"Is that a dare?"

"No," I said. "You indicated you were upset with Peter."

"Upset about what? Peter and I are just friends."

"I wasn't sure."

"Now that's funny." Jules cracked the window. "For a couple of months Peter and I shared a house with a friend from acting class. My car has been in and out of the shop. Peter's between gigs and volunteered to drive me around."

"What about your strange revelation?"

"Oh, we can discuss that later." She looked away as if entranced by the blur of buildings flashing by on Highland. "Tell me about your mission."

I turned west onto the Santa Monica Freeway, the late afternoon sun squarely in my eyes. Everyone complains about Los Angeles traffic, but I have come to accept with a measure of amusement how the traffic ebbs and flows. There is a rhythm to the crazed crush of humanity comparable to the genetically programmed zeal of Salmon as they swim upstream against all odds only to spawn and die.

"Clay has someone he hasn't seen for a long time. He asked me to find her."

"What's the name?"

"Mercedes Cruz. She lives in West Hollywood."

"Let's check it out." Jules engaged her smartphone with a

flurry of dual thumb strokes and scrolling. "There are several. Oh, here's one. She's a singer."

When we exited into Santa Monica I phoned the Royal Dolphin to say I'd arrive in a few minutes. Mr. Lu's eyebrows went on tilt as I walked through the door with Jules in her tuxedo.

"Mr. Sid. How you are?"

"Fine. Thank you. This is Jules Marlow. Jules, Mr. Lu."

"Very good, Mr. Sid." Jules and Mr. Lu exchanged polite bows. He made a note on his clipboard. "Very good, Mr. Sid. Very good."

"Is Mr. Harmon in his room?"

Mr. Lu pointed to the right. "Sitting room. Sitting."

Clay rose from a couch and steadied himself with an ornate walking stick. "And who is this?" he asked.

"Jules Marlow. I hope it's okay that I brought her along."

"Better than okay." Clay squinted. "Nice tux. What's the occasion?"

Jules extended her hand. "A failed costume party."

"I like your style. You make Sid look uptown."

"Do you think so?"

"But that doesn't take much."

"Okay you two," I interrupted. "Clay, I thought you were blind."

"I told you I was 'legally' blind. There's a distinction." He coughed into a fist and cleared his throat. "So, Captain America, what happened with Stanley?"

"We have an address and a telephone number." Clay sat down. Jules and I settled on either side of him. "What's the plan?"

Suddenly Clay was wide-eyed as if he'd consumed two shots of espresso. "Like we talked, we stake it out and see what happens. But let's not mess around. Sunday morning is a good time. Can we go tomorrow?"

Jules raised her hand like a fourth grade student requesting permission to speak.

"Pardon me, Starsky and Hutch, but you boys run the risk of becoming a creep show. Girls don't like stalkers, particularly on Sunday mornings."

"Okay Veronica Mars," I said. "What would you suggest?"

"For the record, I love Veronica Mars." Her voice softened. She turned to Clay. "It would be nice to know the story."

Clay sat up on the couch. Jules held his hand.

"It's okay," she said. "We just want to know what we're getting into."

Clay squinted at me then turned to Jules. "For Mercedes, her mother Marina and anyone else, I'm an old friend of the family. I promised Mercedes' grandmother I'd keep it that way. That's a promise I must keep."

"Fair enough. Give me a second." Jules' ninja thumbs went to work on her smartphone. She showed Clay the screen. "Is Mercedes a singer?"

"Yes, like her grandmother." Clay peered down his nose. "That's her."

Jules scrolled her phone. "She has a showcase tonight at the Truly Tango Lounge in Hollywood."

Clay beamed. "Why not?" he said. "Of course. Let's go."

"Okay," I said. "We're all in."

Jules nodded agreement. "And we have plenty of time to eat," she said. "But first we need to swing by my place. I have to change. It won't take ten minutes."

The sun had set behind us when we parked in front of Jules' stucco building. Clay sat quietly in the passenger seat as she hurried down the sidewalk.

"Why has it been so long?" I asked.

Clay turned away, rubbed the length of his chin. "I don't want your friend to know because this makes me look like a heel." His tone was emotionless. "The last time I saw Mercedes was ten years ago on her sixteenth birthday. Marina threw a party in the back yard. After they cut the cake I had one bite then passed out face first into a slice of angel food. That's what I was told. At first everyone thought I had a heart attack. One of the cousins took my pulse, smelled my breath and declared that I was drunk."

"Why would you do that?"

"It was a low point." Clay looked up at the sky, the feathered clouds pink and twisted in the wilted light. "Booze made me numb. When you're young the drinking is for kicks. Time passes, friends fade or die and then there's love and the damage you do that can't be undone. Eventually everything worth having slips away. All you want is to forget. I preferred to be numb."

"What happened with Marina and Mercedes?"

"Marina didn't banish me, nor will she ever forget. Mostly I regret causing a scene for Mercedes. She's a sweet kid. I've stayed away. After that Lena insisted I get sober. My little sister can be hell on wheels, but I didn't do it because of her. I decided I'd rather feel something, even if it was pain."

"That was the right call."

Jules dashed down the sidewalk wearing a striped sweater, a tie-died pencil skirt, a navy blue beret and her retro sunglasses.

"Ten minutes flat," she said. "What'd I tell you?"

"Now you're a beatnik?" I asked.

"Appropriate attire for our caper." She snapped her fingers like a beatnik at a bongo festival. "Shall we eat?"

No one protested when I suggested Mel's Drive-In on Sunset Boulevard. We settled into a green vinyl booth as Roy Orbison's *Only the Lonely* played on the jukebox. At Mel's I usually sit alone at the counter like a character from Gottfried Helnwein's painting *Boulevard of Broken Dreams*. A print hung in our family den so that image is seared into my brain. Jules ordered the Belgian waffle, for me grilled chicken breast with steamed vegetables and Clay chose grandma's chicken soup. As our server turned away a young woman walked by wearing plaid flannel pajama bottoms, a tank top and pink bunny slippers, her right shoulder covered by an unfinished tattoo.

"Is that girl wearing pajamas?" Clay asked.

"Yes, she is," answered Jules. "That's fashion reserved for a late night run to Walgreens for behavioral meds." Jules removed her sunglasses with a mischievous wink at me on the bench beside her. "Hey Clay, tell us how Sunset Strip used to be."

"Well, we didn't wear pajamas." Clay turned a spoon through his coffee. "I had just begun acting in 1953, the year *From Here to Eternity* won the Academy Award for best picture. In those days you dressed sharp for a night at the clubs. The guys and I loved Ciro's and Mocambo. We had a lot of laughs. Whatever we wanted was ours. The Strip was glamorous like that up until the early 60s when everyone went hip and started wearing denim jeans."

"Wasn't Ciro's where the Comedy Store is now?" Jules asked. "I heard a friend say that it's haunted."

Clay smiled. "That's right and there are many reasons that place would be haunted for me. That is where I met Mercedes' grandmother Maria. She had just begun singing before Ciro's closed in 1957. She had the most beautiful face and an easy laugh, but what a voice. We became good friends. It began innocently enough then, when she separated from her husband, I went for her like a schoolboy."

The server brought our food. Jules dressed her waffle with measured amounts of butter and maple syrup without comment from me. We ate quietly and when we were finished Jules resumed her inquiry.

"What happened next?"

"Maybe Clay has shared enough," I said.

"No, it's fine." Clay cleared his throat. The server took our plates and refilled his coffee. "Maria was reluctant to become involved. One weekend I convinced her to drive up the coast to the Biltmore in Santa Barbara. It was romantic the way things are in the early going. Then I went to New York for a month." Clay hesitated, stared at the blackness in his cup. "When I returned to Los Angeles Maria had reconciled with her husband. She left me the most wonderful note. And that was that."

Jules touched his arm. "I'm so sorry."

"It's alright." Clay smiled, his expression bordering on happiness. "That was a couple of lifetimes ago. Now here we are."

The server brought our check. "Let's move," I said, grabbing the bill. "We have a show to catch."

On the drive to Hollywood I lowered my window and welcomed the rush of the cool night air. We arrived early and took a small table near the bar where we watched the room fill. Eventually the piano player stepped onto the stage. A smooth-voiced announcer said, "Welcome to Hollywood's Truly Tango Lounge and an evening with Ms. Mercedes Cruz." The room erupted with applause. The lights went down for an anxious minute then the spotlights illuminated the fair-skinned Mercedes in a floor length red satin dress, her raven-black hair long and straight.

"What does she look like?" Clay asked.

"I thought you could see."

"Come on, Sid. From here all I know is she's wearing a red dress and has good posture."

"She's amazing, like a Latina Jessica Rabbit."

"A beautiful face," Jules added. "Angelic. Stunning."

Once the applause faded the audience, clearly friends and committed fans, waited in hushed silence. Mercedes cradled the vintage microphone as a mother would a newborn child.

"Thank you so much," she whispered. "Tonight I will cover some of my favorite Cole Porter songs. I hope you enjoy them."

She opened with *I've Got You Under My Skin*. The audience waited spellbound then, with the final note, burst into wild applause. Jules whistled and snapped her fingers beatnik style. This scene repeated at the conclusion of each song. Mercedes embodied the lyrics, owned every nuanced gesture and vocal inflection. During *In the Still of the Night* I looked at Clay. With eyes closed, head bowed and hands clasped, he listened as if a decade of prayerful anticipation had finally been answered.

Mercedes sang *Anything Goes* followed by *Night and Day* and ended her show with *Just One of those Things*. When the final note faded Clay vaulted from his seat, dropped his walking stick and joined the applause. Mercedes acknowledged the pianist and bowed gracefully. When the ovation ended the room buzzed with conversation.

"Come on," Jules said to Clay. "Let's go say hello."

Jules and Clay walked arm and arm. As they neared the stage Mercedes moved out of the spotlight. The instant she saw Clay did not require illumination. The crowd parted. Jules stepped aside as Mercedes wrapped her long arms around Clay's shoulders and pressed her cheek to his.

Each year on Oscar's red carpet, artists and celebrities say how they are in the moment, how everything is surreal and they are honored to be present. At the end of the evening the Oscar winners express gratitude to their peers and to the ones they love. The camera will cut to an adoring spouse or lover, the occasional parent. No doubt they will cherish that moment of recognition, of the love they share for life and how life is more important when they are together. I considered all of this as I watched Jules Marlow turn and walk toward me. She smiled and snapped her fingers.

# Alpha Girl

My battle for beauty began when I was 11 years old. I'm older now, but I remember that day in the middle of winter, the season in Oklahoma when everything dies. My dad and I were driving to pick up Uncle Roger from the Heart Hospital after his triple bypass surgery. I sat in the back seat like a celebrity, like dad was my chauffeur.

"I want to buy makeup," I said. "Some blush and lipstick."

"Why? So you can look like someone else."

"Dad, we're going to the mall." I never call him daddy. It's either dad or Mr. Flores, sir. "We're not Amish."

"Don't be in such a hurry to grow up," he said. "It's overrated."

"Yeah, right. The evidence is overwhelming."

In the rearview mirror I spied a rare smile in the watery depths of dad's dark eyes.

"Maybe lip gloss," he said. "That's it."

Our family is blended. That's a polite way of saying it's broken. Everyone has issues. Strong people just keep going. When I was small my mother loved to brush my hair. "You are lucky Allie," she said. "In sunlight your hair shines like gold, a fine golden blond." Mother understood the nature of beauty, of color and art. She had my ears pierced when I was a baby. I wore her earrings, but only the studs. The dangly drops and hooped hoops were too easily tangled when my hair grew long.

Uncle Roger buckled into the front seat. "Hey Allie, what's it like to be short?" he said. "Do you feel invisible? That adults look right through you?"

"You mean over you?" I said.

After school I watched *Jeopardy!* You learned to ask proper questions, that some people knew better than others. Certain things were true. The rest were opinions.

Roger grinned, scratched his chest like a monkey. "Technically, I'm your great uncle, your grandfather's brother," he said. "You can call me great or the greatest."

"That's not funny. Not even close."

"Tough crowd," Roger said. "Allie, you take after your father."

I retreated into silence, the place I went to gather my scattered thoughts. I knew for a fact that I take after my mother. She died when I was six. Lung cancer. One day she came home from the hair salon coughing. In six months she was gone. Dad doesn't talk about it much. Not since he married Charlene. When I see people smoking cigarettes, like in the parking lot at Penn Square Mall, I want to snap the stupid right out of them.

Uncle Roger checked his gray Frankie Avalon hair, that's what he called it, and flicked the plastic evergreen tree hanging from the rearview mirror.

"Here's some advice for a girl your age," he said. "Never get into a car with an air freshener. God knows what they're hiding."

"Now Roger," dad said.

"I'm just happy to be alive." Uncle Roger started to unbutton his shirt. "Want to see my scar?"

Dad and I spoke in unison, "No!"

"I'm grateful the Heart Hospital is close to the VA," he said. "That kid surgeon did a bang-up job. I promised the cosmetic girls at Macy's I'd show them my scar."

"Do you want us to go with you?" dad asked.

"Are you kidding? You'll cramp my style."

The first Sunday of summer Uncle Roger came over early for our Flores family dinner. He sprawled shirtless in a lawn chair wearing sunglasses, his aged skin slick with suntan lotion. The long pink scar in the middle of his chest resembled a plump worm.

"Sunlight helps to shrink my scar."

I didn't gawk. No one shares photographs of old people on Snapchat. "Look," I'd say to my friends. "It's my great uncle Roger, he's really not that wrinkled."

"Your pretty red hair has gotten long," Roger said.

"My hair is golden blond." I protested. "Only clowns have red hair. I'm not in a circus. I cut it short each summer. I donate the hair for kids with cancer."

Roger, unfazed, put on his Hawaiian shirt but left it unbuttoned. The sliding glass door opened with a screech. Charlene balanced a platter of hotdogs and a bag of chips. Dad carried an ice chest with sodas and Pabst Blue Ribbon beer. Charlene offered me a hot dog.

"They're all natural," she said.

I recoiled. "So is cobra venom."

"Allie." Dad objected. "Don't be a smart ass."

"Allie is too big for her britches," Charlene said. "She's getting bossy."

After mother died I cried myself to sleep most every night. Sometimes dad would read bedtime stories. We talked about going to Disneyland in Orlando. We talked about getting a puppy, too. That ended when Charlene came along. She's allergic.

Uncle Roger chewed his hotdog. French's mustard dripped on his worm of a scar. Dad opened a beer.

"Everyone has their opinion," I said. "If I was a boy you'd call that leadership. You'd call me the boss."

I spent a lot of time exiled in my room that summer. The walls were painted green and pink, the color of wedding mints. A red Japanese dragon kite hung above my bed. Dad and I flew it once on my 11th birthday. Charlene thought the dragon was scary, but I am not afraid. Some days I dressed my Barbie dolls or watched *Jeopardy!* Mostly I colored in my coloring books or read stories about lost girls.

That final evening in mother's hospital room she brushed my hair with long careful strokes, sang *Somewhere Over the Rainbow* just above a whisper. Through the window a full moon rose. "We're guided by the rhythms of nature," she said. "This is a blue moon. It's special, like you Allie, because it doesn't happen very often."

Dad held my hand as we walked through the hospital, the sterile floors polished slick. When we passed the children's ward I saw a girl about my age. No hair or eyebrows. Pale skin. Her wide blue eyes consumed with a faraway look. She reminded me of my mother, and every daughter who ever lived, strong and beautiful in her own special way.

The winter I turned seventeen Uncle Roger moved into the apartment behind our garage. A blended family argument ensued when dad told Charlene Uncle Roger needed a place to stay. She insisted rent be paid and that he help with the gardening. The apartment is a large studio space where my mother planned to paint and style hair. There is a little galley kitchen, a skylight and lots of walls where Uncle Roger hung photographs of his ex-wives and girlfriends.

"Dad has only been married twice," I said.

"Your father is much wiser than me."

Uncle Roger adjusted one of the frames. We have earthquakes that make cracks in the ceiling and send wall hangings wonky. Dad said the earthquakes were caused by directional oil drilling, that they were shallow and won't kill us.

"Why did you have so many wives?" I knew the answer, but liked asking the question.

"I never found the right one." Roger pointed to a young woman with straight black hair. He scratched his chest, the bypass scar hidden beneath his cowl-neck sweater. "This one came the closest. Now I'm too old. All I have are memories."

Uncle Roger hunted for something more elusive than animals, something I did not fully understand. Dad had explained the basics of love and marriage and discouraged me from dating. "There will be plenty of time for that," he said. I have boys as friends, but I'm not hormonal crazy about them like most girls.

"I'm glad you weren't a big game hunter," I said. "The place would be full of bleached skulls and animal skins."

"You're right Allie. It would smell like dead meat."

I haven't eaten meat since sixth grade. We were at the fairgrounds petting zoo when my best friend Rita's mother described the "other parts" of an all beef hotdog. It was totally gross. This cow with sad sleepy eyes stared at us. We felt the warmth of her body and that ended our carnivorous era. Rita's mother reminded me of my mother, sharp and soft-spoken with the poise of a dancer. She shared that Rita and I were Pisces, a water sign, that we're resourceful, empathetic, and sensitive. I don't mention astrology at home. Dad doesn't care, but Charlene thinks astrology is superstition. Charlene, like most people, is afraid of things she doesn't understand.

In Oklahoma the wind is a constant companion, sweeping my hair in all directions, breathing untold mysteries in my ears. Late on nights when the wind didn't blow I listened for the freight train horn and wheels rumble along the Santa Fe line. The tracks are miles away to the east, but I heard the train clearly. While the rest of the world drifted in dreamland I pondered, stared at my red dragon kite and the hairline crack that inched across my ceiling.

In the spring Rita and I began work after school at the Veggie Bowl restaurant. The first Saturday of summer break I had my hair cut. That afternoon Rita and I browsed through the Second Hand Rose resale shop where I found this navy blazer, a military cut with an embroidered floral crest over the heart. I tried it on in front of a full-length antique mirror.

"It's like brand new," I said. "And only twenty dollars."

"A perfect fit." Rita was right behind me. "You should have it."

Our cheerful reflection remained fresh with the new-found freedom that comes from having a job and paying your way. The edges of the antique mirror had begun to fade. What about all of the people who had gazed into this mirror, about their hopes and dreams, if they were dressed for school or a wedding or a dance? In the midst of wonderment, my fingers strayed into a pocket and found a slip of paper that read: Hand made with pride in the U.S.A., February 1999.

"Hey, look at this." I showed the paper to Rita.

"Wow," Rita said. "That's our birth month and year. That's radical to the extreme. This piece was made for you."

"For us," I said. "We'll share it."

I was wearing the blazer when Rita and I found Uncle Roger on the back patio slumped in a lawn chair holding *Daily Word* magazine, chin on his chest.

"Is he dead?"

"He's either sleeping or counting his blessings." I shook his shoulder. "Hey, Uncle Roger. Hey you, wake up."

His blinking brown eyes filled the lenses of his glasses.

"I'm here. I'm here."

"Have you been drinking?"

He blinked, focused on my face. "I maybe had a couple," he said. "I drink a glass of wine or two every evening. It helps me relax and reduces the chance of a stroke."

"You started early today?"

"Maybe a little early."

We helped him to his door.

"That's a good looking sport coat," he said. "And your hair. You look sharp, like an adult. You must be raking it in waitressing at that vegetarian restaurant."

Rita and I smiled. "Yes, we're doing well," I said.

"I wish you worked at Steak and Shake, someplace with food I like."

The next night we had a customary Sunday Flores family dinner. Unlike Rita's clan we don't hold hands and pray or sing a dinner song. We basically eat and talk. Dad grilled hamburgers and a veggie burger for me. I made a mixed green salad with avocado, cucumber, purple onions, walnuts, and sliced beets with lite balsamic vinegar dressing. Dad and Roger helped themselves to my salad and Charlene's baked beans.

"Allie, your salad is delicious," dad said.

"Yes," Charlene said. "So fresh and healthy."

I gave Charlene credit for trying. We coexisted with an unspoken truce since I started cleaning the house, my homage to her and Cinderella. Uncle Roger ate his burger without jokes or offhand commentary, a sign of something awry. He groaned as he retrieved a bottle of Lone Star beer from the ice chest.

"Can you help with this?"

I twisted the cap. He took a drink.

"You know you're old when you need assistance with childproof packaging," he said. "When wine and beer are the foundation of your wellness program."

Dad and Charlene exchanged glances.

"How are you feeling?" asked dad.

Roger took another drink, surveyed the vegetable garden where the sunflowers he planted flourished in front of the fence.

"I go back to the VA in the morning. The doctor's nurse

said there's something going on with my bladder."

"You shouldn't be driving," dad said.

"I can see just fine."

"I'm more concerned with your hearing."

"I hear what I want to hear."

"That's my point. I'll go with you."

Charlene took her plate and went into the kitchen.

"No, you'll miss work," Roger said. "I don't want to bother anyone."

"I'll take him," I said. "I'm off tomorrow."

The next morning Uncle Roger wore his Dallas Cowboys windbreaker. He loves the Cowboys and anything to do with Texas, his state of birth and mind.

"It's almost summer," I said. "Won't you be hot?"

"It's freezing in the VA hospital. You'll see." We climbed into his Ford Escape. "Sure you can drive?"

"I scored 100% on my driver's tests."

"You're exceptional."

I drove east of downtown. The security guard at the VA gate checked Roger's ID then looked at me.

"This is Allie," Uncle Roger said. "My driver."

A few somber patients waited curbside for their rides. Abandoned wheelchairs littered the entry sidewalk. Just inside the hospital, past the photograph of President Obama, Uncle Roger stopped for coffee.

"Do you want coffee?" asked the attendant. "A soda or a donut?"

"No," I said. "I don't do caffeine or sugar."

Uncle Roger and the attendant rolled their old man eyes.

"Girl," the man said. "You don't know what's good."

Serving sugar in a hospital is akin to a dentist dispensing jawbreakers, I thought. Everyone is on autopilot. Veterans and relatives crowded the hallway and the elevator. When we reached the fourth floor urology department Uncle Roger took a number.

"Hurry up and wait," he said. "That's the government way."

We took a seat. Most of the patients were Roger's age. One veteran nearby, wearing a Wounded Warrior T-Shirt, was barely older than me.

On the television a reporter held a beagle puppy. "People are dumping unwanted dogs on isolated roads near Midwest City," the reporter declared. "It's been happening for years. Some of the lucky pets end up in this shelter. They deserve a loving home."

"What are they saying?" Uncle Roger asked.

"People are abandoning puppies."

"Heartless assholes," he said. "Oh, sorry."

"You're okay, that's appropriate. Thoughtless people leave it for others to clean up their messes. It's pathetic."

After thirty minutes the young veteran stood. "I drove two hours for this appointment." He spoke loud enough everyone could hear. "I've waited an hour and a half. I'm done. I'm leaving."

Uncle Roger turned to me. "We should go, too. I'm hungry."

"No," I said. "We wait."

About an hour later they called Roger's number. I stayed in my seat, took deep breaths, imagined the birthday dad and I flew the red dragon kite. On the ride home Uncle Roger didn't speak until he asked me to pull into the Gas and Go convenience store. A man on the curb held a cardboard sign: I NEED A BEER.

"I need one, too." Roger scoffed. "But today I'm buying lottery tickets. My luck has to change."

I didn't ask questions. Dad met us in the driveway.

"How'd it go?" he asked.

"Bad news." Uncle Roger hung his head. "I have bladder cancer, stage four. They want to start radiation, twice a week for sixteen weeks."

Dad helped Roger out of the car. They embraced. I waited and tried not to cry.

The veterans arrived in the radiation reception area with wives or husbands or a friend, someone to take them home. They chatted with nervous energy and pre-treatment pep talks. A few of them prayed. Unknowing, Roger and I sat off to the side. He perked up when the cute young nurse held his arm and led him through the double doors to the treatment room. In the hallway after treatments the patients shuffled along, stooped as if the life had been sucked out of them.

Uncle Roger, pale and drawn, reached for my hand.

"I have you," I said. "Let's take a wheelchair."

"I can walk."

"We don't have all day. Come on, it will be fun."

Twice a week that became our morning routine. During treatments I sketched in my sketchbook or jotted in my journal, listened to Today's Alternative Radio on my iPhone or texted with Rita or my dad. This sweet nurse Darby rubbed Roger's shoulders after she wheeled him out.

"See you next week," he said.

"Roger that." Darby flashed a smile you can't fake. "It's a date."

We'd stop for Roger to buy lottery tickets. Dad or Charlene served his dinner in the apartment. I brought veggie-tofu brown rice bowls from the restaurant. Rita and I worked afternoons and evenings. Off days we'd go for long walks at Lake Hefner or Martin Nature Park, the lush trees full of life and given voice by the breeze. Wild deer roamed the park, grazing and sniffing the air. They kept their distance. Visitors are warned not to feed them or get too close.

Dad assumed Roger's treatment duties once school started. Near the end of September the doctor ordered tests and an MRI. I took off school and went with them to the appointment.

"You're in good shape," the doctor said. "Considering you chose not to operate or have chemotherapy. The cancer has not spread. Let's take a thirty day break and schedule tests and another round in early November."

"That's great," Roger said. "That's just wonderful."

I was concerned he'd start singing or dancing, bust a move with his cane.

"Be cool," dad said. "Control yourself. The reception room is full of people who may not have such good news."

Roger felt stronger after a few weeks. One night when I delivered his veggie-rice bowl he listened to John Coltrane's *A Love Supreme*. I pointed to the wall of photographs, the gallery of ex-wives and girlfriends.

"Which one did you love the most?"

Roger pointed to the woman with straight black hair.

"In Cherokee they don't have a word for goodbye," he said. "She never used that word, but I did. I regret I don't have a legacy, anything to leave behind."

"What about your son?"

"We don't speak. He doesn't want to hear from me."

Roger crossed the room and returned with a copy of *Alice in Wonderland* by Lewis Carroll and a large box.

"These are not much," he said. "But they are things I treasure. I want you to have them."

"If they mean something to you," I said. "They mean something to me."

"Wait to open the box. You'll know when. It's full of letters and pictures I sent home from the war, to your great grandmother and grandfather."

I insisted Roger come along to meet Rita and her six-year old sister Megan at the mall for Trick or Treat. The children dress up, the stores hand out candy. I wore the crested blazer with my hair up under a sea captain's cap. Rita wore a long formal dress.

Roger chuckled when he saw us together. "The Captain and Tennille?"

"If that's what you see," Rita said. "Go with it."

Megan wore a black witches costume and hat, her face painted dark green.

"She's obsessed with the Wizard of Oz," Rita said.

Roger braced on his cane, knelt beside Megan.

"Are you a good witch or a bad witch?" he asked.

Megan bared her teeth in a fierce expression, curled her fingers into claws. "I'm the scary witch," she said.

We cruised the mall, stopped at each store and when Roger needed to rest. At the entrance to Macy's we lingered.

"Do you want to see your girlfriends in cosmetics?"

"Another day," he said. "I'm tired."

The next week I missed school one morning to take Roger for blood work and imaging. In the radiation department Darby set him up with a lab tech to take blood.

"How's he doing?" Darby asked.

"He seems to be fading," I said. "Doesn't eat much. Tires easily."

"Sixteen weeks of radiation is intense," she said. "It takes time to recover. The tech is having issues finding a vein. He's taking blood thinners."

Roger sat slumped in his wheelchair, his face in hands. Darby went over, stroked his back, and looked toward me. I could barely hear.

"I don't want to die," Roger sobbed.

I pretended I had not heard, drove Roger up to Lake Hefner and parked on the east side with an unobstructed view. Sailboats negotiated a brisk autumn breeze under a gloomy gray sky. The leaves on the trees along the walking trail had turned yellow and gold, one by one they were carried away. Roger cleared his throat.

"When I came home from Viet Nam there was no homecoming parade," he said, his voice broken, breathing shallow. "Outside the airport war protestors waved signs, chanted and yelled. This one girl, about your age but nothing like you, I remember her face all warped and red with rage. She spit and called us baby killers. I never killed anyone. I was a corpsman. My job was saving lives."

Sometimes I tune out, my mind wanders and I apply the comfort of silence to my invisible wounds, but I listened to Roger's words as if they were his last.

"There's no sanity in war, no glory. You see young bodies ripped apart, writhing in pain. You try to stop the bleeding, give them a chance with bullets screaming by your head. All we wanted was to survive, to make it through the night, and go home. Soldiers don't forget any of that. Every horrible sight and sound and smell is burned into our brains. That is the burden of our duty."

A shaft of light pierced the gloom and swept across the lake.

"Try to think about all of the lives you saved," I said. "About the life you gave those soldiers and the goodness they were able to share with their families."

"Of course," Roger said. "You're right."

The day before Thanksgiving I wheeled Uncle Roger into the VA for his doctor's appointment. The coffee attendant, ever joyful, stopped us in the hall.

"Thanksgiving is coming," he said. "You have a place to eat?"

Roger nodded. "My nephew's going to feed me."

"What?" The man grinned. "To the dogs?"

"A good one." Roger coughed, scratched his chest. "I'll remember that."

He slapped Roger's back. "Give thanks, my brother."

Dad met us in a doctor's office with barely enough room for Roger's wheelchair, dad and me. The doctor reviewed the file, rubbed his chin.

"This is going to be hard," he said. "The cancer has spread."

Roger sat up in the wheelchair like he was at attention. Dad held my hand.

"In early June we could have operated, removed the bladder and tumors. Mr. Flores declined surgery. We took a chance. The outcome was negative. I'm not sure further radiation will be helpful."

The doctor scribbled out a prescription.

"This should make you feel comfortable," he said.

Thanksgiving night, after our solemn family meal and pecan pie, Rita and I bundled Uncle Roger into the back seat of the Escape and drove through Heritage Hills to see the Christmas lights.

"This neighborhood always has the best decorations," Rita said. "Traditional, but updated."

"Oh, look." Roger struggled to speak, pointed to a two-story house set well back from the street. "I've always loved the blue lights. I don't know why."

"I love the blue ones, too," I said. We parked, watched the lights strung across the trees and hedges flicker and glow. "Blue is cool and moody as opposed to the cheery and bright of red and green. With shades of blue, like in the summer sky or on a lake throughout the day, there's more nuance and subtext."

"Nuance and subtext," Rita said. "Honors English. Listen to you."

When we got home I gave Roger the keys.

"Keep them," he said, his tone unhurried. "The Escape is yours, for Christmas. Unlike me it doesn't have many miles."

"What if you need it?"

"You'll always be my driver."

"Thank you," I said.

"That's so cool." Rita gave Roger a hug. "Merry Christmas."

A few nights later the jet stream fueled a freakish winter storm that roared down from the north with freezing rain and snow. Charlene made turkey noodle soup. Dad and I served Uncle Roger. I played the Indigo Girls' song *Closer to Fine* as we got him into bed.

"Have you taken your medication?" dad asked.

"Yes, but no blood thinners," he mumbled. "Doctor's orders."

Dad placed his open hand on Roger's chest. I put my hand on top of his.

"Sweet dreams," I said. "God bless you."

Roger closed his yes. "Bless you," he whispered. "Bless you both."

We turned off the music and the lights. Dad pulled me close as we walked to the house, the icy snow crunched beneath our boots.

"Allie, I'm so proud," he said. "Of everything you are."

Inside, the kitchen was warm and toasty. I kissed my dad on the cheek.

"I've had a lot of help, Mr. Flores, sir."

In the night the wind laid down and the temperature dropped. A fresh blanket of snow muted the world, quieted my busy mind when it was ready to roam. Off to the east a freight train sounded its horn and rumbled south down the Santa Fe tracks. I considered the lifeline etched across my palm, the notes in my journal, and the stories I would one day tell. Sleep at last carried me away on a bed of carefree clouds.

I awoke at 7 a.m. to hushed voices in the backyard, a police car and an ambulance in the driveway. I grabbed my coat and rushed outside. Snowflakes fell upon my face, big soft ones melted in my tears. Dad wrapped me in his arms.

"Roger passed in his sleep," dad said. "Likely a stroke. All that remains is a body. You don't need to see that."

I did not want to see the shell of his body. I wanted to enter the studio apartment and fill the void with music, play *Radioactive* by Imagine Dragons loud enough the frosted windows rattled in the frames. But there was much to do when someone leaves this world. The mortician came with a gurney. Dad helped him wheel the body to be donated for medical research. Then there was the grief and the realization that in the end Roger had few friends to mourn him.

Rita, my sensitive Pisces sister, comforted me. In my room we organized Uncle Roger's wartime letters and photographs and planned a project to read each letter aloud as if Roger was there, listening. The next Sunday I made a festive mixed green salad with strawberries and invited Rita for Flores family dinner. We set the table with blue placemats and a framed photo of Roger in uniform. Dad, Charlene, Rita, and I held hands. Rita prayed then I sang a six-word song, a tribute to my mother and Roger, all the lives they touched and the beauty to be found in each passing moment: "Thank you. Thank you. Thank you."

Thank you for reading
*Prudence in Hollywood and Other Stories.*

Your Amazon, Goodreads or other review
will be greatly appreciated.

MR

# Acknowledgments

I am grateful to the editors of *Playboy* for publishing *Prudence in Hollywood*, the editors of *American Way* for publishing *The Reunion of Last Resort*, and to Mark Brown, editor of *INFO*, for publishing stories including *The Myth of the California Girl*.

Thanks to readers Melissa Brevetti, LeeAnn Holmberg, and Megan Gentry for your edits and encouragement.

Thank you to the UCLA Extension Creative Writing Program, and instructor Jamie Cat Callan, the Los Angeles Writer's Block including Janet Fitch, Diana Wagman, Cat Bauer, Marlea Evans, Charlotte Laws, and Charles Parselle.

For Myra and Ralph, my mother and father, thank you for the gift of story, your love and example on living a purposeful life. I acknowledge stand-up comedy guru Greg Dean for years of friendship and inspiration.

# About the Author

The author of the novel *Angel City Singles*, Ralph Cissne is an award-winning poet whose short stories have appeared in publications such as *American Way* and *Playboy*. The novelette *Claim to Fame* and poetry collection *Don't Be Shy* were published in 2015.

A native Californian, Cissne grew up in a military family and graduated from The University of Oklahoma School of Journalism. He lives in Oklahoma where he writes and volunteers as a creative life skills mentor.

Cissne is a member of PEN America, The Author's Guild, and a lifetime member of the National Eagle Scout Association.

For more, visit RalphCissne.com